MURDER IS FOR KEEPS

When private eye Mark Preston was hired to chase an amorous musician away from teenage heiress Ellen Chase, it sounded simple. But within twenty-four hours he was beaten up and made the number one suspect in a case of murder. He was also in trouble with wealthy casino-owner Vic Toreno. Dark figures began to emerge from the past, and a sex-killer stalked the streets of Monkton City. Then, showgirl Cuddles Candy gave Preston an unexpected lead — unexpected, because Cuddles had been fished out of New York's East River years before!

PETER CHAMBERS

MURDER IS FOR KEEPS

Complete and Unabridged

LINFORD
Leicester

First published in Great Britain in 1961

First Linford Edition
published 2004

British Library CIP Data

Chambers, Peter, *1924* –
Murder is for keeps.—Large print ed.—
Linford mystery library
1. Detective and mystery stories
2. Large type books
I. Title
823.9'14 [F]

ISBN 1–84395–319–6

Published by
F. A. Thorpe (Publishing)
Anstey, Leicestershire

Set by Words & Graphics Ltd.
Anstey, Leicestershire
Printed and bound in Great Britain by
T. J. International Ltd., Padstow, Cornwall

This book is printed on acid-free paper

Prologue

The moon hung in a smog haze over the Manhattan skyline. There had been rain earlier and the streets reflected wetly the pale yellow light from the sky. It was two in the morning, and everything was still in the neighbourhood as the black sedan moved smoothly round the corner and stopped. The headlights died and the motor was turned off. The car seemed to shrink anonymously into the surrounding darkness. After a few moments the door opened and the driver stepped out into the street, checking quickly in both directions that there was no one approaching. With the gentlest of clicks he shut the door of the car. The collar of his coat was pulled well up about his face and the dark wide-brimmed hat was snapped down over his forehead. As he walked across the street the thick crepe on the soles of his shoes deadened all echoes. He moved lightly and neatly, like

1

a tightrope walker, like a man who was accustomed to moving in the blackness of the night without noise. He was of medium height or less, very thick in the body. It was difficult to be certain in that light, particularly in view of the overcoat, but he gave an impression of being very fat.

Avoiding the well-lit front of the apartment building he walked soundlessly down the passageway at the side, emerging into the small square at the rear. Here were the garages for the use of the apartment-dwellers. The rear entrance to the building was illuminated by one dim light that hung suspended over the doorway. Heading straight across the concrete square, and moving with the assurance of one who was on familiar ground, the fat man stopped before one of the low squat garages. It was just possible in the feeble light to make out the silvered number '6' that was displayed prominently at the side. The hat nodded as if with satisfaction. Edging into the narrow space between the buildings the fat man paused when he reached the small window let into the side. Then reaching into his coat pocket, he withdrew a pencil torch. Shading the light from the apartment-building with a massive gloved hand, he held the torch against the glass of the window. The needle beam of light picked out the windshield of the car that stood inside. He moved the beam rapidly over the body of the car until he was satisfied with his identification, then switched off and returned the torch to his pocket. As silently as he had come, he worked his way back to the concrete square. Leaning against the doors of the garage in a position from which he could observe the rear of the building he settled down to wait. One of the apartments on the second floor was lit up. Heavy curtains at the windows prevented anyone from looking in, but cracks of light all round the edges of the curtains announced that someone was home in Apartment 6.

An hour passed, then another. The fat man seemed almost frozen into immobility at his vantage point at the garage. Occasionally during his long vigil a shadow would pass over the curtains, and this would make a break from the monotonous routine of staring at nothing.

The scream came at ten minutes after four in the morning. There was only one, a high panic-stricken piercing cry, a woman's, then silence. Lights sprang to life in other apartments, heads appeared at windows. Shouted enquiries passed from one to another. The fat man remained perfectly still, confident of the protection of the night. Then, beneath the poor light suspended over the rear entrance a man and woman appeared. Immediately the fat man shrank back into the passage at the side of the garage. Spotting the couple leaving the building some of the heads at the windows turned downwards, calling out.

'Sorry folks, very sorry. Just a nightmare that's all. I'm taking the lady to a doctor. She's given herself a bad shock.'

The man's words carried clearly to the unseen watcher. Prompted by the sudden jerking of the hand holding her elbow, the woman turned her head upwards towards the anonymous faces.

'Sorr-Sorry to wake you this way.'

The show was over. There were some irritated muttering, the faces withdrew, windows banged shut. The man half-dragged, half-carried the woman across the remaining distance to the garage. He inserted a key in the door, and the entrance swung noiselessly up, disappearing into the roof. A light came on automatically and the couple blinked in the sudden glare. The man was young, twenty-five or so. He had an aggressive face, mounted with a mop of dark curly hair. He wore a Tuxedo with a light overcoat thrown across his shoulders. The woman was a pale beautiful creature, who might have been any age between twenty and thirty. Her face bore the marks of suffering, there were huge dark rings beneath her eyes and she moved like a sleepwalker. She wore an evening gown of gold lamé beneath a fur wrap. There were marks all over the front of the gown. Wet marks that showed dull against the shining material.

'Stand there while I get out the car. And for crissakes keep a grip on yourself.'

She remained standing where the young man indicated, eyes glazed over as if in a trance. The car motor roared once, then fell back into a steady purring sound. There was a faint hiss as the brakes were released, then the car backed out. The right hand door was pushed open from inside and the curt voice ordered the girl to get in. She did so, and at once the driver wheeled the car round and moved towards the exit road. There was silence again.

The fat man stayed hidden for a moment. This was an unexpected development. If he hurried he could get to his own car and follow the couple, but he hesitated. Then his mind was made up. Quietly and without haste, he walked to the entrance of the building. Pulling the hat further down and making certain the collar of his coat was as high as it would go he went inside. Ignoring the elevator he made for the carpeted stairway. When he came to the landing he paused listening intently. In the silence he could hear his own heart beating. Finally he reached the door of Apartment 6. The dim light in the hallway struck a glint from the metal as he inserted a key in the door, turned it soundlessly. The apartment should be empty, but the intruder was not a man to take chances. His right hand moved inside the overcoat and came out holding a flat ugly automatic. Then, almost gracefully, he stepped inside. The lights were on and there was no one in the room. Always without seeming to be in any hurry, he closed the door carefully. It was a small apartment. Expensive but small. One living-room, two bedrooms, bathroom, one cupboard-size kitchen. He checked the kitchen and bathroom. Empty. The first bedroom was also empty but there were indications that someone had been sleeping there recently. He prowled around the room, studying, evaluating.

In the second bedroom he found the girl. He saw her as he opened the door, and stopped suddenly, drawing in breath rapidly between his closed teeth. She was on the floor. She was naked except for a cheap bracelet on the right wrist. Her right hand was twisted into the silk

7

bedclothes which she had pulled in her frenzied attempts to haul herself free. Free of the raving maniac who had stood over her slobbering and plunging an eight-inch steel blade repeatedly into her exposed body. The carpet and the nearby furniture were splashed with blood. The head was half-severed from her shoulders.

The fat man drew his tongue over his lips. The hand holding the automatic was shaking. Slowly he got a grip on himself. His life had not been of a kind where he was unaccustomed to violent death. The savagery of the girl's mutilation had set him back for a few moments, but now he was recovered. Now he could think. Putting the gun away in his pocket he began a search of the apartment. He had to be quick and he had to be methodical. The murdered girl on the floor was going to provide him with the kind of situation he had always dreamed of. He was going to be on easy street from here on in.

1

Her name was Moira Chase, and as she sat down in the chair opposite my desk, I could think of several reasons why she might be in the kind of trouble that would bring her to me. She was tall, about five-seven with a full thrusting figure that made a mockery of the severe green suit. Her femininity derided the obvious attempts to conceal it, despite the costly efforts of some high-priced fashion expert. Her hair was nut-brown, pulled into tight waves around her head and disappearing into a bun at the back. Dark, luminous eyes which flashed whenever she raised her head from a demure inspection of the carpeting. Her cheekbones were long clear lines leading to a small but determined chin. She'd tried to make her mouth uninteresting by affecting a dull lipstick, but the restless sensuality of those lips was not to be denied. It would have been no surprise to find woollen stockings on the long tapering legs, but she evidently had decided that would be going too far. They were tanned a golden brown colour. I guessed her to be in her early thirties, but then I never was a guesser. There was a plain golden band on the third finger of her left hand which was getting plenty of advertising.

'What can I do for you, Mrs. Chase?'

The soft brown eyes regarded me thoughtfully. She looked to me the way someone would look if they still weren't sure it was a good idea coming to me.

'Do you know who I am, Mr. Preston?'

The voice was good. She used it to communicate words to other people, not in the hope I might be a talent scout from a major studio.

I shook my head.

'No, I don't think so.'

'I'm the widow of F. Harper Chase. My husband was prominent in this state up to the time he died last year.'

She waited as if to give me a second try at it. It paid off.

'That one?' I replied. 'Why yes I

remember your husband very well.'

F. Harper Chase had been a noisy politician around my part of California ever since I could remember. His death about fifteen months previously had been quite a news item.

'People usually do.' She said it without expression. The words called for a hint of pride, or even bitterness according to the circumstances, but the widow of the late lamented F. Harper Chase might have been buying a bottle of aspirin.

I passed.

'My husband left four things behind. A gap in the political machine, a daughter Ellen, a great deal of money, and me.'

She wasn't just talking. This was a business conversation and I was being given preliminary facts. A look at her expression told me I was entitled to an inference from the last remarks.

'In that order?' I queried.

'In that order. Frank was a real politician, not one of those milk-and-water modern types. In many ways he was a hangover from another era. With him it was politics all the time, not from nine

11

a.m. till five in the afternoon.'

'I never met him, but what you tell me about fits what I remember having heard. You mentioned a daughter?'

She nodded.

'Ellen. She's seventeen now. Any time Frank had left over from his routine went to her. She was the only person he ever really cared for. Aside from himself, that is.'

I must have looked too much like a man who wasn't going to register any kind of reaction no matter what she said. Suddenly she smiled. I liked it.

'Sorry if I embarrassed you, Mr. Preston. You must have thought I came here looking for a shoulder to cry on.'

'No, er, not at all,' I tried but it sounded lame. That was exactly what I had been thinking.

'Perhaps I ought to tell you about Frank and myself. I met him about five years ago in San Francisco. He was fifty then, twice my own age We went out a few times. His first wife had died a couple of years before so there was no harm in it. I liked to eat in nice places, he could

12

afford it and so far as I was concerned there was nothing else to it. Then he made me a proposition. Have you a cigarette?'

I had to wait to find out about the proposition while we fooled around with cigarette lighters and ash trays. She was one of those people who hold a cigarette between the thumb and forefinger all the time.

'Thank you. I was telling you about the proposition Frank made me. It wasn't the kind I'd been expecting.'

I grinned. Mostly to show that it couldn't have been the kind I was thinking of either. She didn't grin back.

'Frank wanted to get married. He wanted somebody who knew how to entertain at his frequent dinner parties and so on. Someone who was also decorative. Of course there were any number of women who could have filled those requirements. Where I got ahead was because I had been a nurse. Frank was very preoccupied with his health. The house was always littered with every horse-doctor's prescription that had ever appeared on the market. There was one more thing. His new wife would have to be someone who took a real liking to his daughter Ellen, and Ellen had to reciprocate.'

'Quite a list of qualifications,' I offered.

'Yes,' she replied seriously. 'Frank was very open about it. I was not the first girl he'd approached. Two others had been ahead of me, one an ex-army nurse and the other an M.D. who wasn't in practice. Neither of them passed with Ellen. Still I don't want to go on too far with this. Merely wanted you to understand my position at the moment.'

Now, at last, we would get to it. Not that I'm complaining. I don't get to sit around making conversation with a woman like Moira Chase every afternoon.

'It's about Ellen that I've really come to see you. As I say she's seventeen now. She isn't beautiful, but she's pretty enough, and when she's finished growing she'll have a very good figure. There hasn't been any shortage of nice boys around the house this last couple of years.'

When she spoke of her step-daughter

there was a warmth in her voice that hadn't been there before. The kind of warmth you'd expect from a girl's natural mother. Frank Chase had known his own business when he made his deal with Moira. She tapped impatiently with the cigarette on the side of the ash tray. A small spray of grey ash settled on the surface of the desk. She didn't seem to notice.

'Now there's someone new. Someone not so nice. Ellen is a great jazz enthusiast. You know the kind of thing, records, concerts and so on.'

I nodded

'She's getting involved with some musician. His name is Kent Shubert and he plays at a place called the Club Coastal here in Monkton City. I believe he's very good.'

The name was familiar. Somebody or other had advised me to catch the new piano-player at the Coastal. According to my information nothing like him had been heard around these parts for a long time. He'd come from the Bay.

'I've heard of him. Somebody told me

he's pretty good,' I confirmed.

'Well, whether he's good at his music or not is another matter. The point is, he's spending too much time with my daughter, and I want it stopped.

Just like that. I doodled with a pencil that lay on the blotter in front of me.

'May I ask just what your objections are to this man Shubert? I mean why do you assume there's harm in this friendship?'

'Mr. Preston, this man is about thirty. Even in the ordinary way I should be suspicious of a man that age who showed too much interest in a girl of seventeen. Remember Ellen is not one of these wild moderns, she's always had a quiet home background, almost sheltered. And remember too that when she's eighteen she'll inherit a great deal of money from her father.'

'Could I ask how much money?' I put in.

'A little over two hundred thousand dollars. As I told you I'd keep an eye on any man of Shubert's age, but when you add the fact that he's a jazz musician, what can I think but the worst? I have known people like him in the past. They live fast, as if every day could be their last on earth.'

I wasn't there to argue with the customers, so I made no reply to that. Instead I asked,

'Just what did you have in mind for me to do, Mrs. Chase?'

'I'd like you to look into this man's history. See if there's anything there that I could use.'

'Use for what?'

'Mr. Preston,' she said firmly, 'I am not asking whether you agree with what I'm doing. I have the responsibility for a seventeen-year-old girl, a girl who is going to inherit a lot of money in ten months time. I don't like her new companion. If I can find any evidence that he's been in trouble with the police for example, then I could use it to persuade Shubert to leave Ellen alone. The police here would move quickly enough if they knew a convicted felon was associating with a girl Ellen's age. Something about contributing to the delinquency of a minor, I believe.'

The phrase was a technical one. Moira Chase had not dreamed it up.

'So you've already seen a lawyer, Mrs. Chase?'

She smiled slightly.

'Oh yes, that was the first thing I did when I realised this state of affairs existed. He advised me to come to you.'

'Who did?'

'Bart Lytton.'

Well, well, we were going up in the world. Bartholomew J. Lytton was one of the most prominent attorneys in the state. If I'd had any doubts about taking the case, I lost them fast. An O.K. signal from Lytton was very beneficial to the credit rating where I come from, particularly with the law.

'All right, Mrs. Chase, I'll get to work on it. You understand I can't promise results, but you'll still get my bill?'

She got up from the chair, smiling.

'That's understood. Good luck, Mr. Preston. You'll telephone me when you have news?'

'Of course.'

I watched her walk across the room, an unnatural stiff-legged gait as if to discourage anybody who might want to think of her as feminine. I wondered about it. Wondered what made a woman with a figure like that want to make herself look almost sexless. For sexless she certainly was not, not that one.

It was almost five in the afternoon. I buzzed for Florence Digby. If Bart Lytton could steer business my way, I could summon enough strength to drop a note thanking him. Miss Digby came in with her book, sat down, laid the inevitable three newly-pointed pencils on the desk by her right hand. Miss Digby is pushing forty-five, and the fact she's stayed single all that time is a tribute to the plain stupidity of the average male. Still attractive, she must have been a knockout as a girl. Her clothes are always well-cut, a little severe maybe, but that's no bad thing around a business organisation. I dug up the business, but it was Florence Digby who treated it in a business-like way. She ran the whole works really, including banking arrangements. Of course she could be a little acid at the end of a long hot day, like now.

'Shall I open an expense sheet on Mrs. Chase, or will this one be on the house?'

The Digby always thinks the worst if I chance to get an attractive woman for a client.

'Mrs. Chase is the widow of F. Harper Chase, none other. She can stand a few expenses, Miss Digby.'

The frosty smile indicated that she was mollified. I wrote a short note to Lytton thanking him for mentioning me, but without referring to the name of our mutual client. Naturally. Then I asked for an envelope, stamped for San Francisco.

'What kind?'

'Medium large.'

I did measuring movements with my hands to indicate the size. When Miss Digby brought it back together with the Lytton letter for my signature I told her we'd call it a day. Then I looked up Joe Armstrong's address in the San Francisco directory. Joe runs an outfit like my own up that way and we were able to help each other out occasionally. I scribbled the address, wrote him a few lines on a sheet of office paper and put the envelope in my inside pocket. I went home.

★　★　★

If the Emperor Nero, Gauguin, Barnum and Bailey had formed a city planning commission they would have come up with something like Conquest Street. Somebody once told me the Conquest bit was a corruption of an earlier Spanish place-name after the conquistadores or some such, and for all I know it's true. I like to think so. The idea of even the name of the street having been corrupted appeals to me. Conquest stretches eleven city blocks from Fourth Avenue clear down to River Street. Respectability-wise that means downhill all the way. Any entertainment you can't find on Conquest Street hasn't been invented yet. This ranges from the legit theatre on the corner of Fourth right down to the kind you first thought of. An endless parade of honky-tonks, pin-ball games, girlie-shows, jazz clubs and bars. Strip joints, clip joints and what-have-you. The lower end, in every sense of the word, is no place to take your aged spinster relatives. By daylight the peeling façades of these rat-holes look dirty and uninviting, but at night the scene is transformed. Everything is glittering and shiny. And uninviting. Monkton is a prosperous town, everybody getting richer every minute. A sleepville twenty years before, then these new defence plants started springing up on every stretch of waste ground. Now the place was jumping. A sudden influx of folding money usually produces something like Conquest Street. Certainly there was always plenty doing down that way. Some of the people in the busy crowds are working joes, barkeeps, waiters and so on. The rest are split down the middle. One half suckers, the other a collection of hoods and hustlers, peddlers, pimps and guys looking for The Man, dames looking for any man. Hookers lounge in every doorway, every side-alley, issuing hoarse invitations to all and sundry. If you have nervous eyes, best keep clear of Conquest at night, where the riotous colour-splotch of the neon-signs is like the nightmare of an impressionist painter.

I hit the street at nine o'clock that evening. The night was rowdy with the clashing of different melodies from a dozen places. Not far away the clean cool air from the Pacific wafted over the city. Here it gave way to gasoline fumes, cheap cigars, a thousand cooking meals. I left the heap in a side-street, locking it carefully. The Club Coastal was a new name for a trap that had occupied the same premises ever since I could remember, under twenty different names. The entrance was a lighted doorway with red carpeted stairs heading down. A neon sign flashed the name of the place on and off. Outside the doorway hung a sign that said Music In Person, Kent Shubert. There was no picture.

As I went down the stairs the conflicting noises from the street gradually died away. There was a muffled sound of music from below. At the bottom I turned into the lighted square that passed for a foyer. A hat-check girl leaned over a low counter. She was a silver-blonde, and was going to need to wear something a little heavier before the winter came on. When she saw me she stood up straight, with a resigned expression.

'Hello, Peggy. New management, huh?'

'Oh, it's you, Mr. Preston. Thought it might be a customer.'

'But I am a customer. You sell liquor here, don't you?'

'Sure, but,' she shrugged, 'you know what I mean.'

'I know what you mean, Peggy. Better luck with the next one.'

The bartender was new to me. I parked on a high stool covered in sickly green plastic, picking a spot from which I could see the whole place. An upright piano stood on a small platform in one corner. A slim man sat there smoking a cigarette and talking to a tall girl in black. He had a lively intelligent face under the bushy dark hair. I made him thirty, or thereabouts. After a couple of minutes the girl went away and sat down at a table. Kent Shubert got rid of the cigarette and turned back to the keyboard. Suddenly there was less noise in the club. Not a complete silence, you never get that anywhere, but enough of a quietening-down to tell me that quite a few people had really come to listen. I listened too. There are all kinds of piano-players. There's the guy who spends all his time producing sixteen notes to every four-beat bar, tearing up and down the keys like an enraged fly. All he proves is how hard he practises his five finger exercises. There's the weirdie who will resort to any stratagem that will assist him to avoid the melody or the original chord sequence. There's the one who spends all his time hammering at an insistent beat, mainly to distract attention from his musical incompetence. Shubert was none of these. He played 'You Stepped Out of a Dream'. The first chorus was nothing special, just a professional musician playing a good oldie, but after that Shubert took over from the composer. He played as though the piano were a whole orchestra, the different sections contributing in alternating phrases. He would build up the arrangement to a point at which the piano could not encompass the range of tone-colours at which he had hinted. Then he would fall back onto understatement, and that was where his genius lay. Instead of feeling a let down at the sudden change, the listener himself was still able to hear the non-existent sections. The listener was involved personally in the orchestration. It was quite an experience. When he finished I joined in the applause, and not just out of politeness.

'Pretty good, huh?'

It was the bartender.

'Terrific,' I nodded. 'Can I buy him a drink?'

'Anybody can buy that one a drink, mister.'

He looked across to where Shubert sat, fingering absently at the black and white notes. After a few seconds the piano-player looked up and caught the signal. Then he eased off the stool and made his way over. He had to stop three times to hear people tell him how great he was. Finally he made it.

'Buy you a drink?' I offered.

'Thanks.'

The bartender had already poured three fingers of rye. Shubert took it in his long slender fingers.

'Here's looking at you,' he said, and drank half of it.

Close to, I could see the restlessness on his face. His eyes were never still, and he had a nervous habit of fingering the lapel of his jacket with his left hand. He was not as tall as he'd seemed when sitting. Around five-nine, and slim all the way up. I doubted if he tipped at more than a hundred and fifty. I also doubted whether the rye was his first today, or even the tenth.

'You like music?' he asked abruptly.

He wasn't really with me. He stood beside me because I was the guy paying for the drink in his hand, but his mind was jumping all over the place.

'Some,' I replied. 'I liked what I heard just now. Especially the first sixteen in the third chorus. Tristano, wasn't it?'

He was with me now. The roving eyes came back and squared on my face. His grin was like that of a school-kid caught fingering the jam.

'You noticed, huh? I do it sometimes. Sometimes when I'm tired, or just plain tired of company. These slobs,' he waved a hand around the club, 'they don't notice. I could play the first two exercises from a Teach Yourself Piano manual. They'd still tell me it was brilliant.'

'Pity, though,' I remarked. 'You're too good to need to steal.'

He made a snorting noise.

'I'm great. I'm sensational. That's why I'm beating my fingers to a pulp in a high society trap like this.'

'You play music for musicians,' I pointed out. 'You must have found that out years ago. You'll never get rich.'

'So I found out. No reason I should like it.'

I let it go.

'What brought you to Monkton anyhow? Plenty towns where there's more appreciation than here.'

'A few. I tried some. O.K. for a few weeks, months even. Then they have to change the show, man. If I was Paderewski I wouldn't beat the system. The customers like to see a change.' He

28

drained the rest of his drink.

'Thanks for the drink. I gotta work now.'

He put the empty glass back on the bar counter and was gone. The management cut down on the lighting expenses in the club and threw a pink spot onto the piano. Shubert sat down, flexed his fingers a few times and went to work on 'Tea for Two'. A flash at the far side of the room told me there was a photographer at work. A cute-looking brunette in fishnet tights carrying a box of flash bulbs slung over one shoulder. She just wandered around clicking the shutter on request and taking five dollar bills from guys who seemed glad of the chance just to talk to her. When she got close enough I beckoned her over.

'How much?' I pointed to the camera.

'Five dollars.' She had a voice like a barker at a fair-ground.

'How long before I see the picture?' I held up a five-dollar bill.

She shrugged her shoulders. At least it started out that way, but a girl built like this one couldn't guarantee the outcome.

I watched the last ripple die away, a long way down from her shoulders.

'Twenny minutes, I guess.'

I held up a second five.

'How long before I see the picture?' I repeated.

She cheered up a little.

'Ten minutes. O.K.?'

'O.K.'

She began to fiddle with her equipment.

'Where do you want to be, against the bar?' she enquired.

'No, it's not me, honey. The piano-player.' I inclined my head towards the pink circle of light.

'Huh? Ten bucks for a picture of a piano-player? You could buy a half-interest in the guy for fifteen.'

She wasn't suspicious, merely curious.

'I'm a music-lover, get it? Go take the picture.'

It took her a minute or so to settle in a position that suited her. Finally she seemed satisfied. The bulb popped, and turning towards me she made an O.K. signal with her fingers. Then she crossed the floor and disappeared between some silver drape curtains. I was so busy listening to what Shubert was doing with just one piano I didn't notice her come back.

'Here.'

She thrust a print in my hands. It was still slightly wet. Shubert had been caught in a moment of turning his head towards the audience and I was holding a first rate replica of his head and shoulders.

'It's good. Thanks, honey.'

I passed over the two fives. She folded them carefully and tucked them inside the camera case.

'The name is Fay. Any time you need another picture. Or just need anything.' She wasn't talking about photography.

'I'll remember, Fay. And thanks again.'

I waited until Shubert finished the number. The print was almost dry now. On the way out I flipped a hand at Peggy, but she was too busy checking hats for a couple of sailors to notice. In the dim light of the stairway I took from my pocket the envelope addressed to Joe Armstrong and stuck Kent Shubert's picture inside. Then I sealed the flap, and went on up to the street. There was a box for night mail half a block down. I slid the white oblong inside.

It was a relief to find the car where I'd left it. Keys or not, a parked empty car is on a short lease of life at that end of Conquest Street. As I rolled uptown I figured I could quit for the day. It was ten-thirty and maybe a night's sleep would do no harm.

I live in a place called the Parkside Towers. Back in the days when I was fresh out of the army, after the Korea thing, I used to say that when I could afford it I'd live somewhere like the Parkside Towers. A lot of us said crazy things in those days. I was lucky. I made it. The building is not beside any park, and fourteen stories is not exactly a tower, but the place provides every kind of comfort you'd expect if you knew the rental. Cars are parked underground, and there's an elevator down there that will take you up to the floor you want. I don't use it too often because I like to have a word with the porter who has the duty in the main entrance. Anyhow I just can't get used to taking an elevator up to the second storey. I slid the car into the bay bearing my apartment number and walked up the concrete ramp leading to the side of the building. The stars were doing plenty of business and the sky had that deep colouring which is more than blue. The moon had not picked up it's full power yet and the light wasn't strong. I was humming a phrase I'd heard Shubert play when I saw the fat man. Quite suddenly he stepped from behind some of the miniature trees at the side of the path. He was expensively dressed and wore one of those Homburg hats, dark coloured. The cut of the suit was spoiled by the way he kept his hands jammed down into the pockets. He had something in there besides his fingers. He may have looked like Wall Street, but when he spoke the voice touched a little nearer home. Like San Francisco Bay, for example.

'You're Preston, huh?'

'That would depend. Who wants to know?'

'It ain't polite to stall when somebody asks a question.'

This was a different voice, and the thing I liked least about it was that it came from behind me. I turned slowly to get a look at my second friend, but he was standing in the shadow of the building. Not so far in that I couldn't see the heavy .45 he was holding in my direction. The barrel looked big enough to crawl down. If he squeezed on that trigger now the left side of my head would be torn off.

'Preston, you're sticking your nose in places that's unhealthy for noses.'

It was the fat man again.

'Really, what places?'

'A big talker. A real brave guy,' he sneered.

He was all wrong. All I was hoping for was enough time for a miracle to happen. It didn't. All that happened was that Fatso stepped a couple of paces nearer.

'Keep your nose clean, peeper. This'll help you remember.'

He was going to slug me. His right hand was leaving its coat pocket and there was a dull glint of metal. You have to be quick and you have to be right. I was slow and I was wrong. I swung around to face the guy behind me throwing out my left hand for the gun. I was probably within two yards of it when Fatso caught the side of my neck with a gun barrel. I stopped moving as a red streak flashed across my eyes. Then something hit me on the right shoulder. I knew, desperately, that I mustn't go down. A boot crashed into my stomach and I doubled up, retching violently. Another foot kicked my legs away from under me and I hit the dirt. I was all washed up.

'I thought this guy was supposed to be tough?'

This was a new voice, a man's, from somewhere far away. It seemed to me I'd heard it before but I was too interested in trying to spit the earth from my mouth. Somebody laughed. I rolled around, trying to pick myself up. Finally I made it in a swaying, half-conscious way. I could make out a shape coming towards me. He lunged at me almost casually. It was a mistake. I used his own weight and a little leverage I'd once been taught out in Korea. He missed the earth and landed on the concrete path. I knew it had hurt him and was filled with a warm glow of savage satisfaction. I tried to laugh but no sound came out. Then a ton weight rammed into my kidneys. The side of the building exploded as I went down for keeps. I hit the ground and rolled over just in time to see a leathered foot flying at my face. I pressed my face into the soft earth and took the kick behind the ear. A great black blanket floated down and I pulled it over me.

How long I was there I don't know. When I started to come round my teeth were chattering with cold. I hurt in places I'd forgotten belonged to me. I was wet with dew, and as I passed a hand carefully over myself I found I wasn't wearing a jacket any more. At the time I didn't care, about that or anything else. I managed to get on my feet at the fourth attempt. Not that my feet were any help. They kept folding up underneath me. The moonlight was brilliant now. I could see my jacket on the ground a few yards away. It took about five minutes for me to reach it. All the pockets were empty. I could see the reflection from metal and recovered the keys to my car at the foot of a bush. All my other belongings were around too, flung about anyhow. The billfold when I finally came around to it, was intact. I had better than a hundred dollars inside in small bills, but my visitors had ignored the money. My head was thumping like a steam hammer, but by now I was standing more or less upright. I figured it was time to go home.

Jack, the night porter, took one look at me and was up from the desk fast.

'Mr. Preston, whatever happened?' he said anxiously.

'Accident, Jack, li'l accident. Too much to drink. Fell over getting out of car. Concrete floor. Accident.'

He looked me over carefully as he took my arm and helped me over to the elevator. I guess I didn't look like somebody who fell over getting out of a car.

'Should I call a doctor?' he asked.

'No, no. No need. Be all right. If you wouldn't mind just helping me upstairs.'

'Sure thing. Surely.'

The poor guy was so anxious to do something he made quite a production out of getting me upstairs to Apartment 6B. The warmth inside the building was making me sleepy. He took me inside. I no longer had the will to stop him doing anything he pleased. He insisted on helping get my clothes off. I guess he did most of the work. My body seemed to be one big ache all over. There was nasty purple bruising on my shoulder and behind the ear where one of my new friends put his leather.

'A nasty fall, Mr. Preston. Look how many different places you got hurt. Did you say it was down a mineshaft?'

I tried to grin. It hurt the side of my jaw so I stopped.

'If you must know, Jack, I had a little argument with a lady I took home tonight. I misunderstood her intentions. She corrected me.'

'Well, O.K., Mr. Preston, I guess it's your own affair. I still think a doctor — '

'Uh, uh. How about a drink though? A stiff one. And help yourself.'

He brought me a man-sized helping of

Scotch, and I put it away fast. It pulled me round temporarily.

'Let me put something on those bruises, Mr. Preston. I got some stuff downstairs — '

'No thanks, Jack. No, I mean it, I'll be O.K.'

We argued some more, finally I convinced him. As he left the apartment he flipped up the light switch. The darkness was good. I lay back on the bed, still holding the empty glass. I guess I fell asleep, if you could call it sleep. I was standing against a wall. A lot of guys were running around practising football kicks. I was the ball. Moira Chase drifted by drinking from a tall green glass. Every time somebody kicked me she cheered. Then the glass turned into a huge revolver. She had to use two hands to hold it. When she had it steady she held it against my ear. Then she started to swear only it wasn't Moira at all, it was Kent Shubert. 'You like Tristano, huh?' he shouted. I took no notice. I was too interested in the huge Alsatian dog which leaned against the wall beside me. The dog smiled. It looked like the fat man. There was a blacksmith with his back to me beating at an anvil with a kingsize hammer. I leaned over his shoulder to get a close-up of the thing on the anvil. It was my head. It just wasn't my night.

2

I climbed up the side of a slimy black ditch. Up on top it was tomorrow. A shaft of sunlight hit me in the face and the back of my head thumped. When I moved everything hurt. I think my back hurt more than the shoulder and my head was worse than my back. Kind of a competition. I dragged myself as far as the shower and turned the wheel to full cold. The icy spray gave me plenty of new troubles to think about, especially round the sore spots. I stayed under till my teeth started to chatter then quit. Wrapping a bathrobe around me I paddled around looking for cigarettes. Halfway through the second I figured I might live. I was even beginning to think straight. Some of the things I was thinking weren't very nice. Like the quiet talk I was going to have with the fat man when I caught up with him alone. Thinking back over the

41

night before I remembered that Fatso and his business associates had taken off my coat and emptied the pockets. They were looking for something, and what they were looking for was a photograph of a certain piano player I could mention. That made it important, for reasons I didn't yet know. They hadn't found it and that made me still important too. When somebody wants something as badly as that they don't give up on one try. I'd be hearing more about that picture. I was beginning to wonder too whether I had the complete confidence of my clients, as the saying goes. If the only wrong move Kent Shubert ever made was to make a play for a seventeen-year-old heiress I was blood brother to a hairy ape. An early talk with Moira Chase was definitely on the programme.

It was now ten-twenty in the morning. I put a call through to Joe Armstrong's office in San Francisco and talked to his assistant, a man named Sloan. Armstrong wasn't expected in the office until the afternoon. Yes, my envelope had arrived and yes, he'd tell Armstrong the deal was hot. Thanking him, I cradled the receiver. Then I cleaned up, got dressed and went out. I was stiff and sore in a dozen places and if anybody offered me a dime I was all set to crawl back into bed for the rest of the day. Nobody was giving away dimes today.

It was a little after eleven o'clock when I left the car outside Benito's. Benito's is a poolroom near the town centre. You probably can't imagine why anyone should want to shoot pool at that time of the day, and the truth is not many guys do. But there are quite a few who use the place as a kind of club. Somewhere to go and chew the fat, pick up a little information, bet the ponies. Benito is a little runt who'd sell his own mother for a sawbuck. He was fooling around with a broom just inside the entrance, making like a working stiff.

'Charlie around?' I asked him.

He leaned on the broom, eyed me carefully, started to speak, changed his mind, then jerked his head towards the stairs. I went on up. The man I was looking for was at the far end of the pool hall, talking quietly to a skinny guy named Mournful Harris. I knew better than to interrupt a private talk. There was a row of empty chairs just inside the door. I sat down and watched the man at the nearest table. He was in position for a very difficult shot. A short fat man with a ragged cigar between his teeth turned from his place at the table, looked me over and said,

'Two bucks he don't make it?'

'No bet,' I told him. 'I've seen him make that play with a baseball bat.'

He shrugged and turned away. The cue-artist looked up, winked at me and pushed the cue lazily. Pockets started filling up all round the table. I grinned.

Charlie Surprise was finished talking now. He stood up, said a final word and walked down the side of the hall towards me. That isn't his real name of course. It started out as Suprosetti or some such but nobody could ever pronounce it properly, or even bother to try. He became Surprise and it stuck, the way these things do.

'You looking for me, Preston?'

'Yeah. Sit down and let's brew it over for a bit.'

He hesitated, then sat in the empty chair on my right. The Hawaiian shirt looked as if it hadn't been near a laundry in six months. If my nose was to be trusted Charlie hadn't been giving the soap manufactures much business for a similar period. But I wanted information and when that's on your list you go to the right market. Which is Charlie Surprise. He knows all about everything and everybody. Where he gets his information nobody knows, but for a fin Charlie will tell you the life history of practically anybody in town. If you spread a ten he'll practically write it out in book form.

'Make it fast will ya Preston? It don't do me no good to be seen talking to guys like you.'

'All right, Charlie. The old Flamenco Bar has a new paint job. It's called the Club Coastal now. Who pays for the paint?'

He swallowed nervously, rolled his eyes and looked fearfully round the room.

'Listen, this is dangerous stuff. Man could grab a heap of trouble just thinking about things like that.'

'Sure, sure. I'll pay for all your trouble, Charlie. And an extra five for the finer points.

I extended three five-spots. He repeated the looking round stuff, then grabbed the bills and tucked them away in his pants pocket.

'I'll see you at the Dutchman's in twenty minutes,' he whispered.

I was puzzled. This wasn't Charlie's normal routine. He always did the scene about the hidden dangers that lay on every side. It's a move to raise the ante, and it usually works. But today he really meant it. Of course it might be an even bigger bluff than usual, because Charlie needed still more money to try to keep pace with his system.

Charlie is a horse-player. He is working on a sure fire system to beat the track and this system uses up a lot of money. The sure fire system had been Charlie's only preoccupation for years now, and the only win he ever had was at Christmas four years earlier when he took Jule Keppler

46

for one hundred and eleven dollars. He bets almost that much every week of the year, but he's an incurable optimist. Naturally. The man is a horse-player. I went to the Dutchman's and sat in a corner booth with a schooner of beer. Charlie arrived soon after, peering around the gloomy bar after the bright sunlight of the street. When he saw me he scuttled over and sat opposite, fingers drumming nervously on the table between us.

'Listen, Preston, you gotta forget it was me told you all this. I ain't got so many friends in this town I can afford to lose any.'

'Relax, Charlie. You know I always protect my sources of information. Now, about the Club Coastal.'

'Toreno owns it.'

'Huh?'

I don't get surprised too easily, but I couldn't figure this one. Vittorio Toreno operated on a smooth scale. He'd only arrived in Monkton a few months before, but already he had a nice operation working up on Millions Mile. It didn't add that he would fool around with a

47

small place like the Club Coastal. On the other hand, it could account for my bruises.

'You sure about this, Charlie?'

'I didn't come here to be insulted. I'm always sure. You asked me something, I told you. That all?'

He half-started to get up, but I put a hand on his wrist. Wearily he sat down again.

'There's more, Charlie. For fifteen bucks there has to be more. A lot more. Or I want my change.'

'Toreno won't like this if he finds out I been talking to you about his business.'

I made no offer. Simply sat quite still, fixing Charlie with a stony glare. Charlie is naturally nervous.

'Well, it's this way. Two or three months ago I get the word Toreno is on the buy. He wants a little place with a liquor licence. It has to be clean, no book, no girls, like that. Just a legit drinking joint with a little music.'

'What for?' I asked.

'Preston, maybe you don't hear so good any more. I just told Toreno wanted to

48

buy in. How's a big guy like him gonna feel if every schmo in town starts asking questions about his business? He wants the place, O.K. he wants it.'

'So what happened?'

'So Ollie Baker hears about it.' Ollie had been the manager of the Flamenco.

'Ollie's been talking about blowing this town ever since they freed the slaves. Anyhow, Ollie mentions to one or two people he'd take the air if only he had a stake of about seven g's. That's a blast, huh? Seven g's for a crummy joint like the Flamenco. It'd be plain murder at five centuries.'

'But Toreno paid up without a squawk,' I said softly.

'Huh? How'd you know? You ribbing me, Preston? You know all this stuff already?'

I shook my head.

'I'm psychic, Charlie. I could tell by your tone that had to come next.'

He looked like a man who'd spent ten minutes building up a story, only to have someone else chip in with the laugh line.

'Like you say, Toreno paid. Ollie

grabbed the dough so fast they say he burned his fingers. He left town, too. But he'll be back, I'll lay odds.'

I wasn't interested in Ollie Baker.

'That's all you know about the club?'

'That's all? Ain't that plenty?' Charlie was aggrieved.

'Sure, it's fine. I'm enjoying your company, Charlie. Stay awhile.' I placed another fin on the table, between his hands. They closed like some flesh-eating South American flower. Twenty bucks was a lot of money to pay out for information, especially since I had no way of telling whether I'd be justified in passing the cost on to Moira Chase. But right now I had a personal interest in things, with marks to prove it. I didn't even mind if I was spending my own money.

'Talk some more, Charlie. Talk about Toreno.'

He peered at me suspiciously.

'You know all about Toreno,' he complained.

'Nobody,' I sighed. 'Nobody knows all about anything, Charlie. Let's pretend I just arrived in town. I don't know anything about Toreno. O.K.? Tell me about him.'

'It's kind of a game, huh?'

'Kind of.'

I was hoping he'd come up with something I didn't know about the gambler. He started slowly, then warmed up when he could see how seriously I was listening.

'Well all right, if you're sure. This Toreno he suddenly hits Monkton six, seven months ago. Came from the Bay, nobody knows why, exactly. No trouble with the cops up that way. Least, nothing more than the usual. But the guy is a wheel, anybody can see that. He has these three guys with him, real pros. They don't talk to nobody, just tag along wherever the boss goes. Not that there's any tiffs with the local talent. The word came down from San Francisco. Toreno is in before he even arrives, and nobody round here wants any hard words with those guys up in Frisco. They play a real rough game.' He paused, 'This how you want it? Sounds kinda silly.'

'It sounds just fine, Charlie. So Toreno

51

gets the glad hand. Then?'

'Then it turns out he's got an operation all set up. One of them palaces up on Millions Mile. He's going to run it as a big-time casino. Everything very high-class, strictly for the carriage-trade. This place is a natural. Great big house in the middle of its own grounds. The grounds are about the size of Texas, so nobody with a badge gets to pay any surprise visits.'

'I heard about the house. How come he was allowed to buy in that section? I always understood the owners up around there had a kind of thing about selling to undesirable characters.'

He nodded vigorously.

'That's right, they do. This gets everybody puzzled for quite a long time. In fact, I don't think many people know how he did it even now.'

He broke off, waiting for me to scratch his back.

'But you found out, didn't you, Charlie? How about telling me?'

'I was going to. It seems the place belongs to Marsland Freeman II.'

He spoke the name with the kind of reverence which is reserved for the kind of money owned by Marsland Freeman II. Not that I'm criticizing Charlie. I can get pretty reverent myself about forty-seven million dollars.

'You're sure about this? O.K., O.K.,' I said hastily, seeing the outraged look coming back on his face, 'You're sure about it. But why? Why should a guy like that do any business with Toreno?'

'Ah,' Charlie looked worried. He always worries when there's anything going on in the world he doesn't know about. 'That's the sixty-four dollar question, Preston. You only gave me twenty clams. Not that I know the answer anyhow.'

'So Toreno moved into the big house, set up his tables, brought some more help down from the Bay, and waited for the suckers.'

'That's it. I hear it's a nice clean game, if you got the fare. Toreno says only pikers cheat the customers. The percentage is all in his favour. He makes a pile of dough, everybody's happy.'

'Then suddenly he does this crazy thing

down at the Club Coastal. What d'you figure on that angle, Charlie?'

'Look, Preston, I already told you I don't know. With me it's crazy. All I know this Toreno is loaded. He has the word from the big fellows up in Frisco. He does business with Marsland Freeman II. If he wants to do something off beat like the thing with the club, O.K. Maybe he's nuts. I should be nuts like that.'

And there was no denying Charlie had a point there. I felt the same way.

'Just one more little thing, Charlie. For you it's easy. I want to talk to a man. He's five-seven, fat, maybe a hundred and ninety. Around thirty-five years old, sharp dresser. I think he works for Toreno. Know him?' He screwed up his eyes and listened hard while I described the fat man. Then his brow cleared and I could tell I'd made a score.

'In one. Little-boy Wiener. Very bad company. They say he used to carry an ice-pick for the syndicate in New York. Yeah, he works for Toreno.'

'But why? Toreno doesn't run that kind

of deal. There's no work around for a guy like that.'

'You know the gambling business, Preston. You buy a deck of cards, make a few dollars, next thing you know some hard guy tries to take it away from you. So maybe you got no work for a guy like Little-boy. You keep him around the house, the hard guys figure it might not be so healthy to muscle in.'

He spread his hands outwards to emphasise how simple his reasoning was.

'Could be. Where do I find Little-boy?'

Now we were on firm ground. Names, addresses, stuff like that. That's how Charlie pays his rent.

'Ferndale Apartments on Chaucer Avenue. Number Fourteen.'

I felt very pleased with life in general, and Charlie Surprise in particular. Now I would be able to have that talk with Little-boy.

'I'm going to make that a quarter, Charlie. For the sake of your own health, better forget you ever heard of anybody named Preston.'

'For twenty-five bucks I could forget my mother.'

He scooped up the last bill. I said,

'I'm getting out now. Better give me at least five minutes before you leave. Better not be seen anywhere near me.'

'Leave? Not me, brother. I'm gonna stay right here and map out the afternoon programme at Santa Anita. By tonight maybe I'll have bought the track.'

I went out onto the sidewalk. The sun was really going to work now, searching out every patch of shade. A green convertible rolled past. At the wheel was a redhead wearing a white dress with no top. She was a gorgeous nutbrown colour, and she eyed me lazily as she passed, headed for the beach. Anybody with any brains in his head would be down at the beach on a day like this, waiting for something like the redhead to happen. I sighed, dug in my pocket for nickels, went into a payphone booth and dialled. I could hear the ringing tone for the best part of a minute before the receiver at the other end was lifted.

'Hello.'

'Mrs. Chase?' I asked.

'Speaking. Who is this?'

'Mark Preston. I want to talk to you, Mrs. Chase. Could I come over?'

She hesitated.

'Could it wait? I mean, is it important?'

'It'll only take a few minutes,' I pressed.

'All right, Mr. Preston. When should I expect you?'

I've talked to people who sounded more enthusiastic than Mrs. Chase. I looked at my watch. It was midday.

'I could be with you in half an hour. Shall we say twelve-thirty?'

'Very well. I'll expect you then.'

Moira Chase's address was a couple of miles out of town, on Muerto Canyon. She hadn't been spilling over with anxiety to see me, and I have a curiosity about things like that. I figured that with the lunch traffic crush I could make it out there in a little over ten minutes. Climbing into the car, I gunned the motor and headed away from the city centre.

3

Muerto Canyon is a crack in the hills about two miles long. In the year 1662 one Captain Hernandez led a sizeable force into the valley. They were looking for gold and other plunder. What they got was a carefully thought-out ambush from the Indians who penned them neatly inside the natural enclosure and fired arrows down from the hillsides from concealed positions. Hernandez didn't have a chance. Up till that time he'd had a bigger reputation for his tussles with the ladies than with opposing forces, but when the chips were down he fought like a tiger, so the story goes. Every manjack of the little army was killed and later mutilated in what was then the approved fashion. After it was all over, even the Indians were appalled at the carnage. The place got a reputation for being the haunt of evil spirits, etc., and everybody gave it a wide berth for a couple of centuries.

Then the wagon trains, pushing on south in the endless trek to Eldorado, began to use the canyon as a natural route. Later, when it got safe for folks to live in isolation, one or two people started to make their homes on the lower slopes of the hills. Then the developers came along and began to stud the whole valley with rancho-style properties. Nothing inexpensive either. Good solid buildings with plenty of ground and a good solid price-tag.

The house I wanted was set back from the highway. A white mailbox had the name 'Chase' etched in bold black letters on the side. I drove on past, found a place to turn, then went back a quarter of a mile towards town. I pulled off the road onto a slight rise and parked where I could watch the entrance to the house. I was probably wasting my time anyhow. All this stake-out routine, just because the woman wasn't thrilled at the prospect of a visit from me. Maybe there was a sex bit in there some place. Maybe it was because Moira Chase was a lot of female, and somewhere deep inside me the hunter was on the prowl. Funny the things you think about sitting in a stuffy automobile on a hot afternoon.

I'd been sitting there for exactly eight minutes when I got some action. A white sedan about the size of an interstate bus suddenly shot out from the curving drive of the Chase house, turned left onto the highway and headed towards where I was waiting. I slumped down in the seat so I was just able to peer through the windshield. The sedan rolled easily along. There was a man driving. He was dark-haired and clean-shaven. He wore a red check sports shirt open at the neck with a few black curly hairs showing. He didn't seem to think there was any reason I should be interested in him, and didn't even glance in my direction as he roared past. He was paying proper attention to his driving. I knew him by sight and wished I didn't. He was going to complicate things for me enough as it was, without being involved with Moira Chase as well. He was Vic Toreno.

There was plenty for me to think about as I sat waiting out the minutes until twelve-thirty. I eased off the brake, coasted down the rise to the concrete ribbon and headed for my client's house. It was a rambling single-storey building with a verandah all round the outside. Built of wood and the local white stone, it looked solid. As though somebody really lived in the place. Too many places these days give an impression the occupants are just passing through.

I climbed out of the car. From an open window a voice called,

'Hi.'

I looked up to see a girl leaning out and looking me over with interest.

She had fair hair, pulled into a bun. The Chase women evidently went in for buns. Her face was long and finely modelled. No beauty perhaps, but a pleasant face. The brown eyes gave a hint of the intelligence that lay behind the smooth tanned forehead. This had to be Ellen.

'You selling something?' she enquired.

'No, I am not selling something. I've come to see Mrs. Chase.'

'Just a minute.'

And she was gone. A moment later she reappeared, stepping through a pair of glass doors onto the verandah. She wore a yellow outfit, bra and brief shorts. The bra was not much more than a knotted handkerchief, and the handkerchief was far from kingsize. Her whole body was just emerging from the schoolgirl into the woman. A woman I should look forward to seeing. In another year that flimsy handkerchief would not be adequate to cope with the impatient young breasts. On her feet were a pair of Mexican rope sandals. Her legs were long and slim, well-shaped and tanned the same rich brown as the rest of her.

'You're Ellen,' I said. 'My name is Mark Preston.'

'Hi, again. Mark Preston.' She rolled it round her tongue. 'I like it. How'd you know my name?'

'Your moth — er, Mrs. Chase told me about you.'

'Moira?' She looked over her shoulder to be sure we weren't overheard.

'What'd Moira tell you about me?'

She was all lively interest, like a puppy

62

waiting to be told he's a good pooch.

'Oh,' I pretended to think about it. 'Let's see. She said you were pretty.'

'Good. What else?'

'She said you were going to fill out into a very attractive woman.'

'Zat so?' She was hugely delighted. Placing her hands on her hips she turned round, slowly and provocatively. When she was facing me again, she said, 'Well, what do you think? Was she right?'

'She also said you were seventeen years old,' I told her gently. 'That about puts you out of my year, Ellen.'

'Oh pshaw,' she pouted. 'You're old-fashioned. Just think, if you grabbed me off now, what a prize you'd have in a couple of years, when I'm full-blown.'

I chuckled.

'A girl like you needs more exercise than you'd get just pushing my rocking-chair. Anyhow, where is Mrs. Chase?'

'She won't be a minute. Told me to look after you. Would you like to sit down?'

She sprawled inelegantly in a garden chair. I sat down opposite her, and took out a pack of cigarettes. Ellen waited to see if I was going to offer her one. I didn't.

'So you knew I wasn't selling anything in the first place?'

She grinned. Her strong white teeth gleamed in the sun.

'Natch. I always ask everybody that. Phases 'em sometimes. Specially if they're very rich and important.'

'I'll bet.'

I was hoping she wouldn't suddenly ask what I'd come about. There was an appealing directness about her that made the prospect of telling her a lot of lies distasteful.

'Ah, Mr. Preston. How nice of you to look in.'

I scrambled to my feet as Moira Chase appeared from another doorway further along the verandah. She wore a simple cut black and white dress. It doesn't sound much when you say it like that, but remember Moira was inside it. She held out a cool hand and smiled. If Ellen had seemed like a kid before, she was more like a babe-in-arms at the side of this poised and groomed woman. 'Good afternoon, Mrs. Chase. Ellen and I were just getting acquainted.'

'So I see.' She turned to her step-daughter. 'Ellen, how many times must I tell you you're getting a little old for sprawling about like that.'

'Huh.' Ellen sat up straight and snorted. 'What a world we live in, Mark. I'm too old for half the things in life, and too young for the other half.'

She treated me to a large wink. I winked back, and Moira wasn't sure whether she liked it.

'What have you two been finding to talk about?' she enquired.

'Oh, the usual. You know, the half I'm too young for,' retorted Ellen.

'You needn't worry, dear,' as a tiny frown appeared on Moira's face. 'He turned me down flat. Didn't you?'

She was certainly a girl for keeping a conversation lively.

'Well, not flat exactly,' I replied. 'More of a delayed reaction I'd say.'

'Flat,' she repeated, turning back to Moira. 'He told me I'd get bored pushing his rocking-chair. Well, I can't stay here all day humouring you old folks. I have things to do.'

She swept off down the white wooden steps and was gone.

'Well, Mr. Preston, can I offer you a drink?'

'Thanks. Anything long and cold would be fine.'

I followed her inside the house. It was cool in there. I took in the expensive furnishings, the kind of heavy stuff that doesn't have much market any more. The whole room made me feel that time would leave it unmarked. Except for a few obvious modernities such as the ivory telephone and electric lighting, the place could have looked very much the same seventy years before, while Moira and I took shots out of the windows at a party of Indians.

She handed over a tall, frosted glass.

'Try this.'

I tried it. There was gin in there somewhere among the ice and the fruit juices. It hit the spot.

'What do you think of Ellen?'

She had seated herself in a high-backed chair. A picture of her that way in the right magazine, and highbacked chairs would have come back with a rush.

'She's a nice kid, I like her. Although I hope she doesn't go around talking to everybody the way she talked to me. Some people might not understand it's just a game.'

Moira nodded thoughtfully.

'I know exactly what you mean. The trouble is I'm not sure just how much of a game it is sometimes. I mean, young people are so unpredictable. Suppose somebody, some man took her literally. Do you suppose that a combination of daring and a feeling of flattery might lead her into any real trouble?'

I shrugged.

'It's possible. She's almost a woman now. I don't see how you can expect to guard her all the time. And, you know Mrs. Chase, Ellen has to find out about the world some time. Not from you or any friend. From a man.'

She pressed the palms of her hands together quickly. It was a brief departure from her usual calm and was soon gone.

'This brings us round to why you're here, doesn't it?'

'I guess it does.'

I set the glass down on a low wooden table.

'Mrs. Chase, we are going to need to be frank with each other if we're to make any progress. Now that I've seen Ellen and talked to her I've got a little better idea of your problem. With her physical appearance and personality Ellen would be a source of worry to any parent. Add in the money and something's bound to happen.'

'Something like this man Shubert?' she asked softly.

'Something like that,' I agreed. 'Although he doesn't appear to be such a bad guy.'

'You've met him?' she sounded surprised.

'Last night. I bought him a drink, and we talked awhile.'

She was giving me all her attention.

'You talked? About Ellen?'

'No. About Tristano.'

Moira Chase was much too self-composed to register anything but the faintest hint of surprise.

'Tristano? I'm afraid I don't quite understand. Is that a place?'

'No, Mrs. Chase. He is a piano-player. The best. Shubert and I talked about him.'

'Really.'

'Yes, really. Bearing in mind what I was doing there — working for you, that is — I thought it might be an idea to have a picture of the guy.'

'A photograph? What for?'

'Mrs. Chase, you asked me to find out the man's history. That means I have to ask questions. People are often bad on names, but show them a good profile or a close-up head and shoulders and you're in business,' I explained patiently.

'Oh, oh yes, I see that. Did you get one?'

'Yes, I got one. Somebody didn't think it was such a good idea,' I watched her face for any sign that might tell me she'd heard all this before.

'You mean he objected?'

'Shubert? No. Not Shubert. Somebody else.' I waited.

'Mr. Preston, I'm afraid I'm not very good at guessing games. What precisely are you trying to say?'

Moira was not so reserved any more. She gave the impression that so far as she was concerned I was being difficult, and nobody was going to get difficult with the widow of the late F. Harper Chase.

'All right I'll get to the punch-line. When I got back to my apartment from the Club Coastal last night I had visitors. Three of 'em, all men. Nasty rough men, not your type at all. They told me I shouldn't be interesting myself in things that don't concern me. They made quite a point of it, even went to the trouble of beating me up.'

'Beating you up?' she whispered incredulously. 'But I don't believe it. I simply don't believe it.'

'No?'

Quickly I unbuttoned the top of my shirt. Then, walking across to where she sat I bent down with my back towards her.

70

'There's a couple of the places where I imagined they hit me,' I told her.

'Oh.' She let out a little gasp. 'Your poor back.'

Then I felt a very gentle touch at the edge of one of my sore patches. Suddenly it didn't seem to hurt so much. She ran her fingers round the outside of the bruises, pressing lightly here and there. When she pressed, I winced.

'But you haven't had any treatment. Wait just a moment and I'll bring something.'

I shook my head.

'No, thanks, it doesn't matter. I'm not much for this woman's touch routine. Just wanted you to see.'

'Now I've seen. Don't be childish, Mr. Preston. Those contusions call for medical care. You forget I'm a trained nurse.'

There was something in the tone of her voice that took me far away from a sunny California valley. The black and white dress became suddenly sexless and more like a starched white apron. Moira Chase was so impersonal I could practically smell the antiseptic. She went out of the room and was back quickly carrying a small white box.

'Sit down there,' she ordered, pointing to an upright chair. 'And take off that shirt.'

I didn't even argue. She came and looked me over.

'I want to apologise for not believing you,' she said softly. 'I'm sorry. It just didn't sound real to me. I mean — that kind of thing — '

'I know. It's O.K., Mrs. Chase. You read about it in the papers, hear it on the newscasts, but it's always somebody else, never you, never somebody you know, I understand how you feel.'

'Thank you.'

Then she went to work, opening up the box and taking out small jars and tubes. She squeezed some stuff out of one of the tubes onto some white gauze and began to smooth it over me. The relief was enormous.

'I think you'll find this will help a little,' she said.

I nodded. It was no time for conversation. All I wanted was to go on sitting there for ever, while she treated me with the jelly. Too soon, the magic movements ceased.

'There, that will do.'

Regretfully I reached out for my shirt, but she held up a finger.

'Not for a few minutes, Mr. Preston. Give the ointment a chance to dry or you'll rub it off on your shirt.

'Oh, sure.'

Now that we'd finished the Dr. Kildare chapter I suddenly felt ridiculous, sitting around half-naked in a room with a beautiful woman who called me Mr. Preston.

'About these three men. What makes you think there was any connection with the photograph of Kent Shubert?'

'After they did this,' I pointed towards my shoulder, 'they went through everything I had, trying to find it.'

'But you were unconscious, surely,' she protested. 'How do you know what they were looking for. It could have been just robbery.'

'Yeah. Except they didn't take anything, including a hundred dollars I had.'

'I see.' Finally, it seemed, she had to accept the idea.

I'd been at a disadvantage long enough, having no shirt on. Taking it off the back of the chair I threw it round me and buttoned it quickly. It was clear from Moira Chase's expression that she didn't approve, but to hell with that.

'Reason I came here today was to find out where we stand, Mrs. Chase.'

'I don't quite follow you.'

'You will. Yesterday you came and hired me. There was a man you didn't like too well chasing your stepdaughter. Could I find something about him that would pressure him off. So I go and talk to the guy, take a little picture. Next thing, three professionals work me over. Why?'

'Really, Mr. Preston, how should I know?' There were two spots of high colour on her cheeks. Finally I was getting through to Moira Chase.

'I don't know how you should know. That's why I'm here. I thought maybe you could tell me. Maybe you think it's the normal thing in a case like this. Well, let me tell you, you're wrong. I'm not complaining about the bruises. They'll wear off. They hurt me, those guys, but it'll wear off. In any case, for bruises I charge extra. But why? When I take on a thing like this I expect the man concerned to take a swing at me. Why shouldn't he? But these other characters weren't in the deal. How about levelling with me, or so help me, I'm through.'

'I don't blame you. I can't ask you to suffer like this. How was I to know?' She lifted her shoulders helplessly.

'You could have found out. You could've asked Toreno, for one thing.'

The colour drained away. Underneath the sun-tan she was pale.

'Toreno?'

'Yeah. Vic Toreno. Real name Vittorio. He's a chum of yours, isn't he?'

'I think you're going a little too far. Yes, all right, I do know Mr. Toreno. That can't possibly have any connection with what happened last night,' she said stiffly.

'Like hell. The top man last night was a colourful character named Little-boy Wiener. He works for Toreno. The Club Coastal, where Shubert works, that's owned by Toreno. The woman who put me onto this trick is a friend of Toreno's. I guess you're right. He hardly figures in this at all.'

Her face was registering surprise. She was even forgetting she was annoyed with me.

'But are you positive about all this? I mean — '

She broke off when she saw the look on my face.

'Now, it's up to you, Mrs. Chase. If you want me out, that's O.K. I'll send you an account plus a little something for the beating. If you want me in, that's O.K. too, but all the way in. I have to know the score. Which is it to be?'

'I want you to stay on, of course. Nothing's any different so far as I'm concerned. I want this man Shubert stopped from pestering Ellen. There's no reason why I should feel differently today than I did yesterday.'

I nodded. It didn't hurt so much as it would have done ten minutes before.

'So I'm in. Now, about Toreno. What's with you and him?'

'Mr. Preston, I'm a widow. Not a particularly old one. I have — men friends. I like to go out occasionally. Vic Toreno is one of the men I date.'

'Not exactly your speed, is he? I don't imagine your solid citizen friends would consider him an ideal partner for bridge.'

'He's a gambler, I know that. I don't consider gambling such a serious crime, Mr. Preston. He's always attentive and considerate, knows how a woman likes to be treated. And as for some of the solid citizens, Vic Toreno is much more interesting than most of them. Since it seems necessary for me to confide in you, I might as well tell you that I consider running a gambling house a lot less criminal than filching the taxpayers' money by building inferior bridges, and hospitals that fall down two years after they're built.'

There was a note almost of defiance creeping into her voice. It was as though she were a character witness at a Senate investigation. Vic Toreno was more to Moira Chase than just one of a bunch of boy-friends. She was telling me that with every word she spoke.

'We could have a long argument about it some other time, if you'd care to. Right now I want to know something else. What's the connection between Toreno and Kent Shubert?'

She looked over at me. Her whole face was more animated than I'd seen it so far. When we talked about Toreno, evidently we were talking about something worth discussing.

'Music. Vic is very enthusiastic about jazz playing. He brought Shubert out to the club one night just so that I could hear him play. Vic does things like that.'

'The club?' I asked.

'Oh not the Club Coastal. The Alhambra. Vic's place. Shubert came over and played. Then another time he came here with Vic. That's how he came to meet Ellen.'

'I see. And did you know Toreno owned the Club Coastal?'

'No, I had no idea till you told me just now. Not that there's any reason he should tell me about his affairs. I'm not a business partner you know,' she pointed out.

'No, I didn't know, Mrs. Chase,' I replied. 'That was something else I was going to ask. All right, so Shubert met Ellen. Then what?'

'They started dating. I think it was all Ellen's idea at first. She would go down to where he worked with a party of friends, just to listen to him play. Then the friends gradually dropped out. Now it's only Ellen.'

'Except that now it isn't only Ellen's idea?' I enquired.

'Oh no. I expect Shubert heard about the money and decided it might be a profitable relationship.'

'Could be. Or he might just have taken a shine to Ellen. That wouldn't be very hard for a man to do, would it?'

'Mr. Preston, I'm not interested in your opinion of Shubert's motives. I want to be rid of him.'

I held up a hand before she could get properly wound up.

'All right, all right. One thing I don't know yet. If Toreno brought the guy here, and is such a friend of yours, surely you could have told him you didn't approve of

Shubert seeing Ellen. He could have stopped it.'

She made a face. Nothing more really than the twitching of her lips, but by her standards it was a face.

'That's the odd thing. I did mention it to Vic on several occasions. But he just laughed at me. Said I hadn't any reason to worry. Old Kent was a nice guy, harmless as a bird. Kept assuring me he would do Ellen no harm.'

'But you don't accept that?'

'No.'

She lifted the lid of a black wooden box and held it out to me. The inside was divided into two compartments. The cigarettes on the left were Turkish, the right Virginia. I was careful to turn right. Then I snapped my lighter for her and noticed once again the uncomfortable position in which she held the cigarette. The Turkish brand were evidently there for her own use.

'Thank you.' She blew the perfumed smoke upwards. It hung in a grey cloud above her head. 'No, I don't accept that. I haven't always had money, Mr. Preston.

Got about a great deal before my marriage, met all kinds of men. A girl develops a sort of sixth sense about men. Just occasionally you come across one who isn't quite right somehow. It isn't anything you can identify, just a feeling, but you learn to trust it. Kent Shubert has that effect on me.'

'But not on Ellen,' I pointed out.

'That's true. But Ellen is not much more than a child. In a few more years she'll be able to spot her own Kent Shuberts. I'm going to see to it the knowledge doesn't come too late. And so, Mr. Preston, are you.'

'Well, it's your problem. I'll handle it any way you want,' I told her. 'About Toreno. Surely a man who goes out of his way to please you ordinarily shouldn't find it too much trouble to steer Shubert away from your stepdaughter?'

'I certainly hoped so, but he wouldn't. And I wouldn't push it too far, because, Mr. Preston,' her eyes twinkled, 'another thing I learned years ago, is that if you spend too much of your time criticising a man's friends, pretty soon there's no man.'

Which was true enough.

'So that's the whole story? Pity you didn't tell me about you and Toreno yesterday,' I observed.

'I'm sorry. I didn't consider it any of your business.' She wasn't trying to be rude. It was just a statement.

'It was my business last night, all right,' I reminded her.

'Yes,' she said flatly, 'I'm sorry.

I got up from the chair.

'If anything develops do I always call you here?' I asked.

'Most of the time there's somebody here who'll know where you can find me.'

She walked with me across the room to the glass doors through which Ellen had emerged earlier. I still had one more point to get across and had been trying to figure the best way of expressing it.

'Mrs. Chase, I didn't come here to knock your friends. The matter you want me to investigate ties in with Toreno at every turn. Maybe,' I continued quickly as she looked like interrupting, 'maybe it isn't him personally. No reason why it shouldn't be someone in his organisation, someone close to him. There's only one way to prevent that someone from being too well informed.'

'You want me to say nothing about any of this to Vic. Yes, I think that's a sensible precaution in view of what's happened.'

She took it well. Her consent was not grudging. Her affairs were drawing interference, and when that happened all bets were off. Including even a boy-friend like Toreno.

There was no sign of Ellen Chase as I walked back to the car and started up the motor.

On the way back to town I stopped off at a roadside lunch-counter long enough to swallow a sandwich and a coke. As I drove into Monkton City I could feel a pleasurable excitement beginning to build up inside me at the prospect of the coming visit with Little-boy Weiner.

4

Chaucer Avenue is one of the new areas
butting onto what used to be the outskirts
of town. Wide and straight, it is typical of
the type of development that followed the
defence plant boom. There are trees
planted at twenty-yard intervals through
the whole stretch, buildings that are new
and yet not so forcefully different from
the originals in the area that they give
offence. The Ferndale Apartments is an
eight-storey block of two- and three-room
apartments in the medium price range.
Most of the dwellers would be moderately
successful business guys, the type who
were two steps removed from the head
man. A quiet respectable place laying back
from the road and with some pretence at
a flower garden running the whole length
of the front of the building. Toreno evidently liked his boys to have a good address.
If Charlie Surprise had correct information about Wiener's beginnings, Little-boy

was moving in different circles to his ice-pick days. Apartment Fourteen was on the second storey. I leaned on the buzzer and waited. There was some shuffling around on the other side of the door, but no answer. I gave the buzzer some more work. Finally a voice said,

'What is it?'

It was the right voice, the voice of the fat thug with the two hundred dollar suit.

'Western Union,' I said in an attempt at a piping treble.

I could hear the scraping of a bolt being withdrawn on the inside of the door. It opened and I was looking at Little-boy Wiener. He was looking down the snout of my .38 Police Special, and his face was the colour of putty.

'Inside, Wiener,' I told him. 'We have some talking to do.'

His eyes never left the gun. Slowly he backed away and just as slowly I followed. With an operator like that, I wasn't going to get the .38 close enough for him to make a grab at it. So I kept it close to my body, watching his eyes for the sudden expression that might signal an attempt to do something.

Thinking about it afterwards I often tell myself that there was something phoney about the set-up, or that I noticed some little thing that told me everything was not the way it should be. All I can swear to is that one second I was holding a gun on Little-boy Wiener at a safe distance of about six feet, and the next second something thumped the back of my head with terrible force, and there was a Chinese pattern rug rushing up to hit me in the face. I wasn't completely unconscious. Hands grabbed me under the armpits and I was dragged across the floor into another room. The door was shut and I was alone. I lay there, cursing bitterly my own fool headedness in not checking behind the door. There was a muffled noise of voices from the next room. My head was thumping too much for me to make any sense of external sounds. I was in a bedroom. Grabbing hold of a chair that looked reasonably solid I clambered to my feet. The guy who hit me must have been a novice at the trade. He hadn't caught me exactly right or I'd have still been on the floor. I was weighing up the chances of doing an escape through the window when a thunderous roar crashed out in the next room. Then there were two more reports. Finally the last echo died away and there was silence. I waited, pressing myself up against the wall behind the door, waited to see whether my turn came next. After about a minute I tried the door handle. They hadn't even bothered to lock me in. Slowly, very slowly I inched the door open. The outer apartment door was wide open. I stepped back into the main room. An awful wheezing sound was coming from my right. I turned to see Little-boy rising from a chair. His hands gripped the sides as he pushed desperately to lever himself upright. His face was contorting with the effort and all the time the wheezing noise came from his throat. The white shirt was a ragged horror across his chest where three slugs had torn their vicious way inside him, and a red froth bubbled from his mouth. The life was draining out of him fast, but his strength was amazing. Somehow he made it to his feet. I don't think he could see me. I think his eyes were already dead. Suddenly he flung out his right arm in a final bid to deny that this could be happening to him. Then he moved his left foot forward as if to walk across the room. The shifting of balance was too much for his failing strength. As the foot left the floor his vast bulk suddenly teetered forward and he fell full-length. He knocked over a small glass table as he went down and the sharp splintering sound as the glass hit the floor made me jump.

I knew I had to get out of there fast. Then I spotted the .38 lying over beside the outer door. I reeled across and bent over to pick it up. There was a sharp stinging smell and a nasty little feeling crawled around in the pit of my stomach. Mechanically, knowing the answer already, I shot out the clip. There were three shots missing.

'Drop it or I'll kill you.'

He meant it. I dropped the gun, and turned towards the voice. It belonged to a young patrolman in the khaki summer uniform of the Monkton City Police. His eyes were hard and narrow as he stood inside the door, blue-black revolver held steadily in my direction.

'All right, turn and face the wall.'

I knew the routine. I faced around holding my hands above my head, palms pressed against the wall. Quickly he ran his left hand around me.

'There's nothing to find,' I told him.

'Shut up. Sit down, over there.'

He waved towards a chair that stood in a corner. There was nothing close by that could be grabbed and flung, no window to dive out of. This guy had been listening at the lectures. I went across and sat down.

'O.K.,' he nodded. 'Who are you?'

I told him who I was.

'And this guy?'

He pointed to the heap of dead flesh that had once been Wiener.

'Name of Wiener.'

'Uh huh. Why'd you kill him?'

'I didn't kill him,' I said wearily. My head was banging still.

His voice became, if possible, even more unfriendly.

'Look, Preston, I want jokes I watch television. Why'd you kill him?'

Suddenly I was very tired. Tired of people pushing me around, banging me over the head. I was sour on the whole world. All I wanted was to crawl into a hole someplace and sleep for maybe ten years.

'Look, officer, I know you feel pretty good. Grabbed a dangerous killer practically in the act and stuff, but lay off, huh? Go out and scribble a few parking tickets.'

'Listen, you — '

He took a pace forward, then checked. A grim chuckle came from the tight lips.

'I guess you'll be taken care of, loudmouth. You won't be walking so tall a coupla hours from now.'

'Great. Now why don't you telephone the Homicide Detail? This is their affair, not yours.'

'My partner already called them. You won't find those guys as gentle as me. Tell you what, make a confession right now and we can keep this deal in the precinct. Those Homicide boys can get awful nasty.'

I ignored that.

'Do you know if Rourke has the shift?' I enquired.

'Captain Rourke? You know him?' He wasn't quite so sure any more.

'Better than you, officer. He's not a captain. He's a lieutenant. His title is Captain of Detectives but his rank is lieutenant. Monkton City pay-roll doesn't run to a rank of captain in the Homicide Detail. When you've been on the force a while you'll get to know these little things.'

'Huh? That all true?' Now he was definitely puzzled. When I made no reply to that, he went on, 'This on the level about him? Wiener here. You telling me you didn't do it?'

'I'm telling you. I'd rather be telling John Rourke. Does he have the shift?'

He consulted his strapwatch.

'Yeah, I believe he does. Today he swings two till midnight.'

That was a relief. John Rourke was an old acquaintance. I don't use the word friend because it is one of the facts of life that a private licence operator can never really be a friend to a regular police officer. There are too many points at which their views and loyalties conflict. But if it were possible, Rourke and myself would be friends. He wouldn't like the set-up and he'd give me a hard time, but at least he wouldn't throw me in the tank just because I had a private licence. There were one or two who would. Another patrol officer arrived. This one was pushing retirement, and his face was expressionless as he looked at Wiener's corpse, then turned his gaze onto his partner, who tried to look as if he wasn't posing for the news hounds.

'Homicide are on the way,' said the newcomer in a bored voice. 'He give you any trouble, Hansen?'

'Uh, uh.' It was clear from the firm negative that my captor was not going to relinquish his position too easily. He was Johnny-in-charge all right, and no gun-crazy hoodlum was likely to get the better of him.

The newcomer gave no sign that he was impressed. Thirty years of corpses and guns had inured him to situations like this. And to eager young patrolmen.

'What's your name?' He was talking to me.

'Preston. Mark Preston.'

'You hurt, Preston?'

Before I could answer, Hansen cut in with,

'No, he's not hurt, Ed.'

The older one turned to him.

'You examined him, huh?'

'Examined? No, there wasn't need. I talked to the guy. He's not hurt.'

'So you talked to him,' the voice was heavy with irony. 'I guess that qualifies anybody for service in Alaska. I talked to Timmy Regan for an hour after I picked him up on a peddling rap. Then he just dropped dead right in front of me. You want to stay a patrolman as long as I have, you want to let the same thing happen on one of your pinches. You hurt, Preston?'

'Just a few bruises,' I told him, 'but thanks for thinking of it.'

He gave a curt nod. Hansen had been deflated considerably at having been found neglecting his duty. The trouble with these theoretical coppers, the one place you can hurt them bad is in the rule-book. He said,

'That's on the level, about this Regan?'

'On the level. He'd been knifed in the stomach. He knew we weren't far behind him, so he stuffed up the wound with rag and tried to make it to the border.'

In my present situation all I needed was a few of these little reminiscences to while away the time. Another two or three minutes went by without anybody saying another word. Then the boys from headquarters arrived. No one paid me any heed. The room was full of people measuring things, dusting every surface for prints, flash bulbs going off like Halloween. The police M.D. and another guy knelt beside Wiener. It looked like chaos, but I'd seen this particular chaos before. Every man there knew exactly what he was doing and was doing it expertly. When they pooled their information there'd be a lot of reading for the investigating officer. Last to arrive was that same officer. I noticed Hansen pulling his cap into shape and then John

Rourke walked in. His eyes raked around the room taking in everything. When they got to me they narrowed slightly.

'Preston? What's he doing here?'

Hansen stepped in front of him and made like a wooden soldier.

'Hansen, sir, Patrol Car Twelve, Fourth Precinct. I found this man at the scene of the crime and held him for questioning.'

Rourke listened carefully while Hansen went into his routine about how he got the emergency call and so forth. When he was through, Rourke said,

'Thank you. Better stick around a few minutes. I may need you.'

It was clear from Hansen's face that he thought he rated more than thanks. Nobody seemed to understand what a hero he was. Just then his partner came back into the room.

'Ed, Ed Caine,' said Rourke, smiling right across his face.

Half the guys there stopped working to get a look at this man who caused John Rourke to smile.

Caine grinned back and took the outstretched hand.

'Hallo, Lieutenant. Been a long time.'

'You bet it has. Must be all of three years, huh?'

'About that. How are Alice and the girls?'

'Fine, just fine. Mollie too I hope?'

'Gets a little trouble with her back these days, but mostly O.K.'

Hansen stood by in amazement while the two men talked. He didn't know that they'd been rookies together back in the early thirties. I'd never met Ed Caine before and it wasn't till Rourke spoke the name that I realised who he was. The thirties were noisy times for young police officers, and these two had made quite a name in those days. I was beginning to wonder whether Rourke was going to talk to everybody in town before he got around to me. Finally he walked across to where I was sitting. Jerking his thumb towards the bedroom he said,

'We'll talk in there.'

I followed him. Inside he sat on the bed, pulling from his pocket one of his noxious little Spanish cigars.

'Shut the door and sit down some-place,' he told me.

I shut the door and sat on the same chair I'd used to help me up on my feet earlier. He took out a match and flicked it with his thumbnail. A cloud of the pungent yellow smoke eddied from between his teeth and swirled around him. He looked around for somewhere to park the match, settled for a cardboard waste bin that stood near the bed.

'What's this all about, Preston?'

He didn't look at me, but that didn't mean he was unaware of the slightest change of expression on my face.

'Am I under arrest?' I asked.

He took the cigar from his mouth, held it in front of him and studied it thoughtfully. When he spoke his voice was soft. Dangerous soft.

'Preston, we had a little fire up on the North Side last night. Three people are dead. The lab boys say it was arson. That means homicide. Three homicides. Now it seems I got another.' He flicked his fingers and a spray of dark grey ash floated from the cigar and drifted towards the floor. 'Since two o'clock yesterday afternoon I have been off duty exactly one hour. For breakfast and a shave. Three unsolved homicides on my desk. Another case I don't need. But I'm the duty officer, so it's mine. You're mine, too. Now, I can heave you inside and be too busy to question you for maybe a week. I don't want to do that. You've usually got a story. I won't like it, but I have to hear it. Like I say, I don't want to spend the taxpayer's money feeding you, but if you stall around with me now, so help me I'm not even going to mention your name again until Wednesday of next week. Let's try again. What's this all about?'

He meant it. I've been in jail before on less excuse than Rourke had.

'There's not too much to tell,' I began. 'I don't even know this Wiener. Last night I went out — '

'Where'd you go?'

'Just around. A drink here and there, you know. Drifting.'

'No, I don't know. Drifting where?'

I named a few places. Busy places,

where the crowd shifts every few minutes, where one more face would go unnoticed. He held up a hand.

'So you drifted. Then what?'

'I headed back to the apartment early. Thought I'd catch a good night's sleep. Where I live, the cars are garaged underneath the building. I thought I'd walk round to the entrance and just have a word with the night porter before I went up. That was when I got jumped.'

'Jumped?'

He raised an eyebrow and looked me over carefully. I laughed.

'Oh, there's nothing on view. These guys have worked before. Everything out of sight to the general public.'

'Make me a privileged character. Show me some places that are off limits to the general public.'

I did the thing with the shirt again and got up so he could see my new back decorations. Rourke grunted.

'Very pretty. So you got jumped. What was it all about?'

'Just a mugging, I guess. First off, this fat guy gets in front of me, then two others went to work from behind. They didn't take long over it. Next thing I knew it was the middle of the night. I was plus a few lumps, minus one hundred and sixteen dollars.'

'So you called the police, huh?'

He knew I hadn't called any police, never would under those circumstances.

'No, I didn't want to bother the police with a little case of mugging. I figured I could probably take care of it myself.'

He cheered up all at once.

'Fine, fine. Now we're getting some place. You recognised the fat character as Wiener, called around this afternoon and blew some holes in him. That's great. You wanta call a lawyer?'

I tried to suppress a grin.

'Well, no. Not just yet. You see it didn't happen exactly the way you figure.'

He tut-tutted, tongue against his teeth.

'Dear, dear. That's a shame. Still, I expected a little more.'

'Here it is. I didn't know the fatso but I got a good look at him. This morning I asked around if anybody knew somebody who fitted the description.'

'And it came up Wiener?'

'Exactly.'

I went on to describe what had happened from the time I arrived at the Ferndale Apartments. Rourke puffed furiously at his cigar, chewing vigorously at the other end at the same time. By the time I was through it was a tattered ruin.

'You want me to buy this, Preston?' he said, when I finished.

'That's the way it happened, Lieutenant,' I replied.

'You won't object if I ask a question?' Without waiting for objections he went on, 'The guy who figured Wiener for this mugging last night, did he have any idea where Wiener fitted in?'

'Told me they called him Little-boy. He was doing a little work for Toreno.'

'A little work for Toreno,' said Rourke heavily. 'You better get out and dig up some new sources of information, Preston. A little work, yet. Wiener practically lived in Toreno's pocket. Look at this apartment. You know the rental?'

When I shook my head he continued.

'Well, I'll tell you. It's two hundred and

ten dollars a month. Pretty fancy for a guy who relies on a little casual work mugging people in back-alleys, wouldn't you say?'

'I hadn't thought about it,' I replied.

'Think about it. And think about this. According to my information which I like to think is a little better than your information, this Wiener draws something like five bills a week for the little work he does for Toreno. It's only natural a man like that is going to risk a jail sentence for picking up a few extra clams from drunks.'

I didn't say anything. My story, weak as it was, had one shining advantage. I could prove nearly all of it, except what happened in Wiener's apartment after I arrived. And Rourke had known me long enough to realise Wiener's murder was not my kind of play.

'You wanta tell me any more, Preston?'

He had to ask, so he asked. He knew that was all I was going to say.

'I know it looks bad, but it's all true.'

'Huh.'

Rourke slid off the bed and prowled

around the room, thinking. I didn't do anything that might disturb him. With the mood he was in I was still not clear of the risk of being detained under suspicion of murder.

'Preston, I'd be lying if I told you I like the story. I know it'll check out, but I don't like it. There's something else here, something we haven't yet got around to. I've been a working copper thirty years and a man gets to know a little something about people. If there'd been another gun, or if Wiener had even a knife I'd have said you killed him. You'd be on a one-way ticket to the gas chamber right this minute. But, fool that I am, I know you didn't just shoot him down in cold blood. I'm going to let you go. Maybe I'm getting too old for this job. I ought to retire. The arresting officer finds a dead man one minute after the killing. He also finds a second man holding the murder gun. So I let the second man go. And don't thank me,' he cut in as I started to speak. 'Don't thank me. You can thank yourself for the co-operation you've given this department in the past.'

'I headed for the door.

'Oh, and Preston.' I stopped. 'If you hear anything about this that might interest me, you know the number.'

'Check,' I said.

I walked past the boys from the Detective Division, still busy with their various pieces of equipment. Hansen and Caine stood close by the outer door, talking. When he saw I was about to leave Hansen stuck out a hand as if to stop me. Caine said, 'Forget it. This guy is not for us. Be seeing you, Preston.'

'Not this way, I hope. So long, boys.'

Outside, I was surprised to notice, nothing had changed. Four police sedans were lined up at the kerb, but aside from the prowl-car none of them showed any badges. A woman in a white dress stepped along on the other side of the street exercising a poodle. A kid on a bicycle passed, hands stuck deep in the pockets of his faded jeans, guiding the machine with his knees. There was nothing in Chaucer Avenue to tell anyone that a fat muscle man named Little-boy Wiener had been shot to death in the middle of this peaceful afternoon.

I went to the office. Miss Digby was on her dignity.

'Give me a break, Miss Digby. The reason I'm so late I've been busy being a suspect in a matter of first-degree murder.'

Which was true.

'Who was murdered, Mr. Preston?' She couldn't keep the curiosity from her voice.

'A very fat man named Wiener. With my own gun. Let me have the keys, please.'

She handed over the office keys and I went into my room. The bottom drawer of one file cabinet is always locked. I found the necessary key, inserted it and slid open the drawer. Inside was a .38 Police Special, blood brother to the one the law boys were now holding. This was no time for me to be walking around relying on my strong right arm to defend me. I checked the weapon and was once again pleased to note how it paid off to keep it oiled and clean. That was at least one good thing I'd learned in the service. I relocked the drawer and stuck the gun together with an extra cartridge clip in my jacket pocket. There was only one major disadvantage. My new friend was not checked out in my name at the Records Division. One licence one gun. I was now carrying an unregistered firearm and that made me just as liable to heavy penalties as any hoodlum. Returning the keys to Florence Digby, I said,

'Oh, and get me Joe Armstrong on the phone, will you?'

As I turned away from her desk she called me back.

'By the way a strange thing happened this afternoon.'

She stopped and waited so I said,

'Really? What was that?'

'A woman telephoned and asked for you. I told her you weren't here so she said it didn't matter anyway. She'd probably got hold of the wrong Preston.'

I sat on the edge of Miss Digby's desk. 'Go on.'

'Well, I asked her what Preston was she looking for, so she described you. At least she described you closely enough that there was unlikely to be another Preston who looked that much like you.'

'Uh, huh. Then what?'

'I told her the description would fit you, and then she said, 'Oh, thank you', and hung up. What do you suppose it was all about, Mr. Preston?'

'Beats me,' I said. 'I daresay she'll call back if she wants to see me about something. Incidentally I collected a few bruises last night. Debit those to Mrs. Chase's account.'

'Certainly. For how much?'

'That'll depend on the final total. Not less than an extra hundred anyway.'

As I stood upright one of the lumps on my back gave me a not-so-gentle reminder. 'Make that one fifty,' I corrected.

Ten minutes later Joe Armstrong came through from San Francisco. After the usual courtesies I asked him,

'Say, how about my boy? You dig up any little thing?' Armstrong pretended to be annoyed.

'Listen, Preston, this is no penny-ante

outfit like that one-man band of yours. This is a high-power operation. I had this guy tagged by one of my investigators two hours after we got the picture.'

'So I'm impressed. What's the answer?'

'You had one half right. The guy was a piano-player. Up here his name was Kenny Napoli. A fair performer on the black and white notes so I'm told.'

'Any record? I mean anything at all. Even a speeding offence would be something.'

There was the sound of sheets of paper being turned over. Armstrong came back.

'This guy is clean. Not a very desirable character but he's clean.'

I felt let down. When I first went for Moira Chase's pitch it had been just another job. But since the beating, and meeting Ellen I'd been hoping Mrs. Chase was right. I just couldn't figure a nice kid like that with a sour musician who was so many years older. So I kept fishing.

'What's so undesirable about the guy?' I enquired.

'He drinks too much and he's unreliable. You know the kind. Works like a good boy just so long. Then every now and then he ties on a big one and nobody sees him maybe two, three days.'

'Kind of tough on his employers,' I put in. 'Does he have a bad name with the agencies for that kind of thing?'

'No agencies involved with this bird. He worked exclusively for Toreno. You know, Vic Toreno, moved down your direction not so long ago.'

'Could be a little something there,' I suggested. 'What's so important about this Shubert or Napoli that Toreno would stand for that stuff? I hear tell he's kind of an exacting employer.'

'Can't say. The file don't run to it. The one sure thing is that Toreno is a great fan for jazz piano, and in his opinion this Napoli is the greatest.'

'Evidently. The guy is still working in one of his joints, here in Monkton.'

'Zasso? Well, I'll note it down. May come in some day. That's about all I got, Preston. Anything else I can do?'

'Yeah.'

I knew Armstrong's prices were in the fantasy class, but I decided to plunge a little on this one.

'About Toreno,' I continued, 'you must have enough paper on that guy to throw the pulp market off balance.'

'Just about. You wanta see it?'

'No. Ninety per cent of it I can imagine for myself. Could you put one of the office people on to making me up an outline of the guy's history? A few names, dates and places all in the right order might be something for me to read on these cold evenings.'

'You bet. Let's see, what's the time now?' Brief pause while Armstrong looked at his watch and summed up the job in his mind. 'I think I can get it off to you tonight. You'll have it first thing in the morning.'

'Fine, thanks.'

We told each other what old friends we were and cut the connection. As soon as I let go of the receiver the bell pinged again. It was Miss Digby.

'There's a Mr. Toreno on the line. Shall I put him on?'

'Sure.'

While I waited for the call to be switched through I realised that I'd been stalling over Toreno. We had to meet some time, and now he was making the first move. Moira Chase had promised not to mention me to him so that angle could be excluded. Yet there he was. Why?

'Preston?' came the enquiry.

The voice was deep, almost musical. It could have belonged to one of those persuasive characters on the ads. who were always sympathising with you about how bad you're feeling.

'This is Preston,' I confirmed. 'You're Toreno, huh?'

'I am Mr. Toreno, yes.' He sounded a little hurt about it. I love guys who call themselves Mr., anyway. 'Look, Preston, we ought to have a little talk.'

'What would we talk about?' I returned.

His tone became a little less musical.

'Listen, peeper, don't talk that way. I don't like it when people talk that way to me. All I want is just a friendly talk. You'll find I can be a very easy man to get on with.'

'I'm kinda busy right now,' I answered. 'Maybe next week — '

'Not next week. Tonight, Preston. At my place, the Alhambra. Do you know where it is, out on Palmside Boulevard?'

'If you want to be mistaken for a native of this fair city Toreno you'll have to learn about the local customs. Palmside Boulevard is known as Millions Mile around here.'

'I'll remember. In case I ever want to be a city councilman or any of those things. Tonight. Around nine.'

'You're crazy,' I told him. 'I don't want to talk to you at all. Even if I did I wouldn't come out to a big dark house in private grounds to do it. You could bury a hundred guys like me and nobody would ever notice.'

'Very funny. Why should I want to do you any harm? Have you done something to annoy me?'

He was being clever now. I could almost feel him patting himself on the back.

'Who knows? People with a lot of business interests can be very touchy.'

Quite suddenly he got bored with the conversation.

'I'll pay for your trouble. Nine o'clock, the Alhambra. If you're a nervous type guy, bring the Chief of Police and arrange for television coverage. All I want is talk.'

And I was holding a dead phone. I fooled around with a notion that maybe I wouldn't go to the Alhambra at all. Just to show Toreno there were people in the world who didn't sit up and beg when he snapped his fingers. That would be a very smart play.

I also made a mental note to ask somebody whether the Alhambra insisted on tuxedos.

5

It was eight-fifteen in the evening. I stood and admired myself in the mirror in my apartment. Pretty sharp, I fancied. The white jacket had made a hole in my wallet at the time I bought it, but it looked like a million dollars. Which was more than I paid. The guy on the selling end told me it was the new material. There are so many new materials I don't even remember the name, but whatever it was, it worked. One more tweak to the tie and I was about ready to leave. The law hadn't returned my gun, but I could shoot just as well with the spare. Not that I was going to get a chance. As I slipped it under my arm I knew the .38 and I would part company at the front door of the Alhambra. The first thing that would happen when I arrived would be a frisking. Exit the .38. So why bother? Because, as an old con-man once told me, if people are looking for something, let them find it. Then sell 'em the other half of the mine. The big half. One of my prize possessions is a small lethal instrument known as a derringer. This little beauty is just three inches long but it will kill somebody very dead indeed if pointed in the right direction. With it goes a soft leather strap and holster. Shrugging my left arm free of the jacket I set about fixing the little weapon around my left forearm. It lay there, snug against my watch. There was a device to prevent it slipping out of the holster when the arm was hanging downwards. I jerked the arm a few times to be sure nothing went wrong. Then I put the white jacket back on and practised plucking the gun out with my right thumb and forefinger. Finally I had it settled just right.

Before leaving I tried calling Moira Chase. The burring noise at the other end kept on telling me I was going to get no reply. It was my fourth try since seven. I wanted to tip off Moira not to look too surprised if we ran across each other at Toreno's place. She wasn't supposed to know me. I gave up trying.

Traffic was not heavy as I headed east out of town. Within fifteen minutes I was rolling along Palmside Boulevard, better known as Millions Mile, was first laid by the Spaniards. They were going to build a straight road, Roman-style, clear across the continent, but after about seven miles they gave the continent best. Being the only proper road within hundreds of miles, this little piece of territory was quite sought after by the folks who had money enough to own horse-drawn carriages and so forth. Their women folk would take the air in style, complete with fans, parasols and what have you. So it gradually became an accepted thing that the best people lived either side of these few miles of paving. Now, long after the gold rush had brought fine roads leading every which way out of Monkton City, the tradition was maintained. Man could work his whole life long and not wind up with sufficient money to buy enough ground there to bury himself in. Aside from the price there were other restrictions on buying in. Various nasty

116

little discriminations against would-be purchasers, which would not stand examination in a court of law, but which held nonetheless. That was what made it all the more surprising that anyone like Marsland Freeman II, the archtype of privilege and inherited wealth, should have let a man like Toreno get into a property on Millions Mile.

After one or two tries I found myself at the entrance to the private road I was looking for. There was a white board, with the name Alhambra picked out in old-fashioned black iron lettering. Thirty yards up the road my lights picked out gates ahead. I slowed down, stopped and waited. Not long. A man appeared from the trees on the left. He was wearing a white tuxedo too.

'Good evening, sir. Just the usual membership check?' He was very polite.

'Not me, friend. I couldn't meet the dues. Toreno wants to see me,' I replied.

'I see. Your name would be — ?'

'Preston. Mark Preston.'

He leaned on the open window next to

the driving seat and had a good look at me.

'I'm expecting a Preston. Anything else, aside from you, that says you're him?'

I fished in my pocket and came up with a driving licence.

'O.K.' He nodded, satisfied. 'No offence, but you understand. Can't be too careful with a deal like this.'

He inclined his head over his shoulder to indicate that the deal he referred to was the Alhambra, and not any private deal I might have with the boss.

'Sure,' I answered. 'O.K. to go through?'

'Help yourself.'

He waved his arm and the gate opened slowly until there was room enough for me to drive through. That meant another man somewhere out of sight, the one who operated the switch to break the electric lock on the gate. If I came out of the joint in a hurry, there would be at least two to cope with at the last fence. A peek in the mirror showed the gate swinging shut behind me. There was a blaze of light now through the trees, and soon I had the house in view. The moon wasn't risen yet so I could only judge the place on the lights that shone from a number of windows. It looked like a large private house full of guests for some weekend frolic. The only touch that marred the picture was the arrowed sign reading 'Car Park'. I followed the arrow into an enclosure, where there were thirty or forty cars ahead of me. Backing around I left the heap pointing to out, in case out was what I should suddenly want. There was a well-lit pathway from the enclosure to the side of the house, which led through a Spanish garden, so far as I could make out in the gloom on either side. Up four stone steps and I was onto the marble terrace that seemed to run all around outside. A man and woman in evening dress were sitting in a trellised arch up against the wall of the house. We all pretended not to see each other and I met no one else on my way to the front entrance.

A pair of wrought-iron gates were fastened back against the wall. I walked between them to the heavy front doors. As I looked around for something to press or bang the doors opened silently. A man stood in a discreetly lighted hallway.

'Mr. Preston?' he enquired.

'Yes.'

I stepped inside. So the boys down on the road had a telephone to the house. The place was guarded like Fort Knox. In the wide hallway there were doors leading off either side. A couple of them stood open and I could hear voices and the tinkle of glasses. At the end, a wide staircase led to the upper floors. It was thickly carpeted. My new friend motioned me towards the stairs and I walked in front of him. From below I could hear a woman's laughter, and wished I'd been given a chance to look through those doors. At the top of the staircase we hit another hallway. This wasn't brilliantly lit either. The deep pile of the carpeting deadened our footsteps as we headed for a door on the far side. My escort hadn't said a word all the way. He was a very large man, the kind who would do most of his talking with his fists. I wondered whether he'd been one of the two men with Wiener the night before, but I hadn't seen enough of either of them to make an identification. When we reached the door he opened it and waved me inside, then followed me. I was standing in a small room which was bare of any furniture or fixings. Just four blank walls and the inevitable carpet. The big guy smiled almost apologetically, took an automatic from his pocket and said,

'The rod.'

That was all. Just like that. And held out his hand for it.

'Say what is this?' I protested. 'Toreno said a quiet talk, no quarrels. Now, first off, somebody starts waving a heater in my face.'

He shrugged the massive shoulders expressively.

'Don't blame me, Jack. Rule of the house. No iron.'

Again he held out his free hand, clicking his fingers. With a great show of reluctance I undid my jacket, pulling the side of the coat well open so he could see what I was doing. No point in having him misunderstand a movement and scrambling my brains all over the wall. He noted all this with evident approval.

'That's what I call sense,' he nodded, tucking my gun inside the waistband of his pants. 'Boss'll see you now.'

We went back into the hallway. Two doors along he tapped with his fingers and waited. Somebody said 'Come in.' Opening the door the gun collector indicated that I was to go in.

I walked past him. This was a different proposition to the last room I'd been in. This was elegantly furnished, and not by somebody with Toreno's taste in elegance. For a fleeting moment it occurred to me that Moira Chase — ? Not that it mattered right then. What mattered was the enormous mahogany desk and the man who sat the other side watching my entrance.

In the car that morning Toreno had looked like anybody else. Well, maybe not just anybody. But fairly ordinary, a strong looking man of evident intelligence, and not one who'd have a lot of trouble finding a dame. Tonight was different. This was his background, the private office with the big desk, cut off from the

122

suckers by walls and a network of hired help. The maroon jacket, the big cigar clamped in strong fingers. The little finger carried a ring with an emerald the size of a pea. The whole place reflected the forceful personality of Vittorio Toreno, who hadn't travelled all the way up from his origins by any other method than his own efforts. Crime is like any other business. The big guys, the winners, have to possess the same kind of ruthless purpose they would need to succeed in a more acceptable profession. You don't get to be a Toreno just by the exercise of muscle, there's more to it than that, plenty more.

He waited until I was standing across the desk from him before speaking. The door behind me had already closed softly and we were alone.

'You're right on time,' he said.

'You wanted to see me?' I replied.

'Yeah. Pull up a chair, you'll find they're comfortable. They ought to be at those prices.'

I pulled up the nearest and sat down. Toreno nodded.

'Fine. Cigar?'

He pushed a cedar-wood box towards me.

'Go ahead,' he pressed. 'You don't get a chance to smoke a cigar like those every day of your life. Havana. I have 'em made up special.'

I let the box lie, took out a pack of Old Favourites, lit one and said,

'All right, so we're big buddies. What'd you want to see me about?'

His eyes narrowed. He hadn't liked the bit about the cigar.

'Look, I'm trying to be nice to you, but you gotta co-operate.'

'Why? I'm not doing any business with you. Not yet anyway.'

'So we'll talk business,' he said heavily, leaning both elbows on the table and staring at me hard. 'You knocked off a guy who worked for me this afternoon. Why?'

'Where'd you get that?'

'Never mind where I got it. Why'd you do it?'

He was not threatening. There was nothing in his tone but interest. We could have been talking about the store where I bought my neckties.

'If you're talking about Little-boy, what makes you think I did it?'

'Huh,' he snorted. 'That's a laugh. I'm a big detective, that's why. Somebody shoots off a cannon, a prowlie cop walks in the door, you're standing there holding the cannon, Little-boy's dead on the floor. I don't say I'm any brighter than anybody else, but with me you get the top spot on that programme.'

'Cops didn't think so,' I pointed out.

'Cops.' He waved a derisive hand. 'Don't tell me about cops. Anyway, there's only one cop in town who wouldn't lock you up on sight for the shooting. That cop happened to be there, and you're still walking around. Way I hear tell, you and the copper are all palsy.'

One thing about talking to a thug like Toreno. He wouldn't be able to understand any motive that hadn't got a large profit content, but let him think there's graft involved and he'll believe almost anything. Right now he was thinking Rourke was the kind of police officer who would fix things for the right people. Me being the right people at present. I grinned knowingly. Toreno was triumphant.

'O.K., O.K., so that's the set-up. And don't be scared to tell me about Little-boy. Don't imagine I'm arranging any little trips for the guy who did it. Sure, he worked for me, but that Wiener was a pain the neck. I ain't even gonna send a wreath. So how about it, what was your beef with him?'

'It was just a personal thing. We had kind of an argument last night.'

'What about?'

'I don't know,' I told him. Then seeing the disbelief come into his face I carried on, 'That's straight talk, I don't know. I went out for a few drinks. When I got home this Wiener was waiting outside. With two other guys.'

I noticed quick interest then.

'These others, what'd they look like?' he interjected.

'I don't know that either. They stayed in back until it was time to start swinging. After that I don't remember much at all.'

'It's crazy. Did you know Little-boy?'

'Uh, uh. Never laid eyes on him till last night.'

Toreno leaned across and pushed a buzzer on the desk. I made sure my back was not turned to the door when it opened. The man who'd taken my gun came inside and stood, waiting.

'Find out where everybody was last night,' ordered Toreno. To me he said, 'What time?'

'Around ten-thirty,' I told him.

'Make it between ten and eleven. And I want to know fast.'

The big man went out quietly.

'Why do you want to know?' I asked.

'I want to know everything,' replied Toreno. 'Any of my boys are out I should be told about it. They're paid to be here. And another thing, nobody working for me gets mixed up in this kind of play. Private wars yet. I got enough troubles without these mugs making any more.'

After that he lapsed into moody silence. An old-fashioned German clock that stood in a corner forced its ticking on my ears. It was beginning to sound like a blasting-drill by the time the bodyguard got back with the answer.

'Well?' snapped Toreno.

'Everybody was here, boss,' was the reply.

'You sure about that?'

'Yeah. Everybody checks everybody else. It's a busy time on Tuesday nights. We'd all notice if one of the guys went missing.'

Toreno nodded.

'I guess so. That's about what I figured. O.K.'

The other turned to go, stopped, faced around again and said,

'Except Little-boy that is. You know he was — '

'Yeah, yeah,' he said. 'O.K. I know about Little-boy.'

With the mention of the late lamented Little-boy, the bodyguard threw me an interested glance then went silently out.

'So it wasn't anybody from here?' I remarked.

'I didn't think it would be. Just checking. I check everything. I didn't figure any of these guys would mix in a deal like that. Little-boy now, he was different. Wrong different. The guy was a pain.'

'So he must have got his talent from somewhere else. Somewhere in town,' I reflected.

'Could be,' said Toreno matter-of-factly. 'It won't take long to find out.'

'I don't get it.' I was puzzled. 'If it wasn't anybody working for you, what do you care who beats me up?'

He laughed shortly.

'You don't read me, Preston. I don't care if anybody beats you to death with a chain.' He sat back in the chair, making himself more comfortable. 'You gotta look at this from my point of view. I got a nice little thing going here. Practically legit. Nobody bothers me, I don't bother nobody. But I do have to have an organisation. Big payroll here, and the help like to think the boss is looking after them.'

Now it seemed clearer.

'You mean, if I knocked off your boy, the other mugs around here will expect something done about me?'

He looked pained.

'Please,' he protested. 'I'm a gambler. That stuff is for trigger-happy farm hands in the Middle West. In the ordinary way, that is. My interest in you is this. If you killed Wiener, and I say you did, I got to show these guys Wiener was on his own time. That's all.'

'You mean you have to show them Little-boy wasn't carrying out your orders when he beat me up.'

'I can see where you must be a great detective. Sure. If a guy is working for me and he gets killed, then I'm supposed to follow through.'

It made a queer kind of sense.

'You could do me a little favour,' I told him, 'when you dig up these muggers, how about telling me who they are?'

He split his face with a wide grin. His eyes were not amused.

'Two guys who beat up a private dick? You must be nuts. If they watch their manners when they talk to me I might even give them a bonus.'

'Thanks, for nothing. Well,' I got up, 'if there's nothing else you want to ask me — '

'I guess not. Stick around the Club a while. It'll take maybe a coupla hours to find out who worked you over. You can see the spot I'd be in if I just let you walk outa here before my business associates know the whole story.'

'Is the liquor on the house?' I enquired.

'I'll leave word,' he assured me. 'There's nothing to get excited about. Just stick around, have a few drinks. I'll let you know when it's O.K. to leave.'

It sounded harmless enough. Toreno couldn't be very worried about me. In the club I'd be mixing with his patrons, and he'd go to a lot of trouble to avoid any strong-arm tactics in front of them. If he was up to anything more than he was telling, it would be less bother for him to keep me right where I was.

He gave the buzzer another push. The big man came back in.

'Take our visitor downstairs, Al. He's going to look over the place. I'm buying the drinks.'

As I walked back to the staircase with Al, I realised I was hoping that it wouldn't prove too difficult for Toreno's contacts to come up with the names he wanted. I had enough on my hands as it was. In the entrance hall, Al said,

'Help yourself. Both these are bars.' He pointed to two open doorways on opposite sides of the hall. 'But — er — don't leave without saying goodnight. Boss wouldn't like that.'

'Don't worry,' I replied. 'I won't go without my property. And you're holding that.'

'Yeah.'

I stuck my head in the first of the open doors. The room was decorated like a Viennese beer-garden. A waiter in knicker-bockers and a long white apron was serving beer in tall glasses to a party of four who seemed to think it was all a good idea. They were the only ones in the place and I didn't have any desire to increase the business. I went across the hall to the other door Al had pointed out. This was a much bigger affair, and an intermittent neon sign flashing over the barkeep's head announced that this was the Broadway Bar. It was busy, about two-thirds full and everybody seemed to be having a good time. Garishly lit, the red and yellow walls were well sprinkled with life-size photographs of cooch-dancers, crooners, strippers, all the trades that everybody associates with the Great White Way. The whole décor was designed with an eye to just one thing, impact. And of impact there was plenty. Everybody seemed to be shouting, trying to make themselves heard above the noise level of the ragtime music that was being piped over the speakers that were dotted about. The bar itself was a deafening assortment of multi-coloured glass. Behind it a smooth-looking charac-ter was busy speaking into a pink telephone. Nobody seemed to take any notice of me as I wandered in. There was no reason they should. So far as I'd been able to check in one quick glance around, there was nobody present I knew. I eased my way between the people at the bar. The bartender was waiting for my order.

'Manhattan,' I said.

'Yes, sir. You'll be Mr. Preston?'

'I will,' I confirmed.

He produced the drink in record time.

It was exactly right, as I told him.

'Thanks,' he grinned. 'Have another? The big boss says it's on the house.'

I took a second helping and wandered over to a small table which was empty. There was a dish of pretzels on it and I began to work my way through them. My ears were getting accustomed to the noise now. Instead of being just a general babel I was beginning to be able to identify some of the voices with the speakers. They seemed an ordinary enough crowd. I gave up long ago trying to establish the backgrounds of people when the only information available is the clothes they wear for leisure. Too often it turned out that the professional criminal I'd been able to spot immediately was the vice-president of a national company or such. These people tonight, however, had more in common than a drink in the Broadway Bar. They were gamblers, and whatever they might do to turn an honest dollar outside the Alhambra, the compulsion that drove them to the green-topped tables was the same. Vic Toreno had known what he was doing when he installed the brassy music in the bar. The insistent four-four quick tempo was calculated to produce an effect of acceleration in the conversation. And the drinking. I could almost feel the excitement building up. Your gambler with a session in view, begins, consciously or otherwise, to anticipate the pleasure to come. Perhaps pleasure is not the word I'm looking for. Stimulation might be better. I could feel it in the Broadway Bar. People were talking too loud, too fast, too much. Soon they would be at the tables, where the hard-eyed dealers waited. The dealers were not on view in the bar. They were probably having a quiet cup of coffee in another room. Somebody once told me that if the money lost on private gambling in a single year could be handed over the Government, federal taxation could be eliminated. These, and other irrelevant thoughts, were buzzing around in my head when a voice said,

'Hello. Do you mind if I sit down?'

A girl was standing at the other side of my table. She was taller than most, with rich tawny hair catching the lights as she moved her head. The evening gown was a creamy yellow affair, close fitting all the way up and finishing just the right side of the regulations. Her shoulders and throat were honey colour. The only make-up on her face was lipstick and with that skin she didn't need any other. Her lips were full and red, smiling now to reveal the white even teeth. She held her head slightly to one side and waited for me to answer. I realised I was taking too long over it.

'I'm afraid that if I say anything you'll disappear,' I offered.

The smile widened slightly and she chuckled, a warm throaty sound.

'Then I take it you've no objection.'

She sat down. Her movements were graceful and smooth. I knew right away that this was no ordinary female. The Broadway Bar would have a special fast exit procedure for dames on the prowl. She was no bar pick-up. She was beautiful, exciting, self-possessed. She was trouble.

'Lady, I don't know how long this dream will run so I'm not going to offer you a drink. It would mean leaving the table.'

136

She liked it. I got the chuckle again only this time I was close enough to see that the amusement extended to the flashing green eyes.

'I just finished a drink anyway. However, a cigarette would be nice.'

As she stretched out her hand to the pack I held I could see that there were no encumberances on the tapered brown fingers. Like rings, for instance. A slim bracelet encircled her wrist, and unless I was mistaken, the large stones set at intervals all around the platinum setting were diamonds. Which would make it quite a lot of bracelet.

'You must be wondering what I'm doing here,' she remarked.

I shook my head.

'No. I don't care what you're doing. You're here, and I'll settle for that.'

She examined my face quizzically.

'You're rather nice. Not at all what I expected.'

'Oh, did you expect something? I mean, did somebody send you looking for me?'

'Not exactly.'

She looked around. The table I'd chosen had the advantage of being set slightly apart from most of the crowd. The chattering groups at the bar were out of earshot too, especially as one of the loudspeakers was conveniently placed on the wall in the gap between us. There was nobody to hear us.

'I knew you were coming here. That is I knew someone was coming. Someone Vic Toreno didn't regard as a blood brother.'

'Really?' Quite apart from everything else about her being interesting, she had a good pitch into the bargain. 'If it'll satisfy your curiosity, I'll tell you who I am. The name is Preston.'

'Thank you. I'm Lois Freeman.'

She said it as though it meant something, so it had to mean something. I dug around in my name-bag.

'Freeman,' I repeated. 'The only Freeman I know of around here is the guy with the private uranium mine. Marsland Freeman II. You wouldn't be related to all that money, would you?'

She nodded, face serious now.

'Yes, I would. I'm his daughter.'

'On the level?'

'On the level.'

This was one for the record. I was sitting three feet away from a beautiful girl who was heiress to one of the largest private fortunes in the country.

'Well, O.K., Miss Freeman, you win the trick. So I'm speechless. What do we do now?'

'Mr. Preston, I want to ask you about Toreno. What your business is with him, why there was so much interest among his employees about your coming here tonight.'

She said it all with a straight face as though she really expected an answer. As gently as I could I said,

'Look, Miss Freeman, we're not going to get anywhere like this. Now, you seem to be interested in my affairs. I'd like to think it was because of my fine manly physique, but somehow I doubt that. You want information from me, O.K. I may tell you, I haven't decided yet. But first you have to put up your end. In other words, what makes me so interesting?'

The ash receptacle was a tiny replica of

the Palace Theatre. She tapped her cigarette thoughtfully against the façade.

'I'm interested in everything and everybody to do with Toreno. Particularly anyone who looks like causing him any trouble.'

The tone of her voice indicated plainly that Lois Freeman would be in there pitching for the guy who blew out Vic Toreno's brains.

'You don't like him, huh? Why?'

'I can't tell you that. It's a very personal thing. You'll have to take my word that it is so.'

And that seemed to be the end of the explanation. I shook my head slowly.

'No deal,' I replied. 'If you hate the guy so much, how come your father let him move into this place? I hear he's not the usual run of tenants.'

'I'm afraid I can't discuss that either.'

We were getting no place at all at a good speed. I tried again.

'You're not telling me very much, are you? Give me one good reason why I should tell you anything at all.'

She bit her lip. She could tell from my

tone that I meant it.

'How would you like a thousand dollars?' she asked. It could have been 'how would you like a cigarette', only it wasn't. It was a thousand dollars.

'Lady, I would like a thousand dollars. Are you offering to give it to me, and if so, for what?'

'To tell me what you're doing here. Everything about Toreno that you know.'

There was no mistaking from the eagerness of the tone that she wanted to know very badly. I discounted the money. To her it was carfare. I felt bad about turning it down, and turning down such a dish as Lois Freeman, all with the same movement.

'Sorry,' I said.

'I don't understand you, Mr. Preston. A couple of harmless questions, questions that you could answer in seconds probably. Yet you refuse a thousand dollars. Why?'

I took another pull at my drink. It was getting warm in the stuffy atmosphere of the bar.

'Let me tell you something, Miss

Freeman. It may help you to understand. I'm a private investigator — '

'A policeman?' she barged in.

'No. Not a policeman. Private cop. I get a licence but no badge. I have clients. People come to me with things that trouble them, I try to put the things right. You've probably heard of the breed, without having encountered a specimen before. Encounter one now.' I tapped myself on the chest importantly.

'Someone, a client, has hired me to do something. Whatever it is I'm doing has a connection with this place. So I'm here. You want me to answer your questions, but you tie in with this place too. So maybe you're involved in my client's affairs. Maybe you're not even on the same team. You can see where I wouldn't be doing any favours for my client if I sat here and told you something, even without realising it, that might be to that person's disadvantage. So you see it's nothing personal, Miss Freeman. It's a business matter.'

She nodded. When she did that the tawny hair bobbed around in a tantalising sweep. To a dame like this I should not be talking about money.

'I can see your position. A business matter. A thousand dollars is a business matter, wouldn't you say?'

I sighed. I'd had similar conversations before. In this romantic, unselfish world the buck was something that got waved under my nose at regular intervals.

'I guess there's no point in continuing this. You don't understand my position at all. You say the words but they haven't any meaning. What I'm trying to get through to you, Miss Freeman, is that I'm hired. The cab is engaged. You're a knockout, and I don't mind if we just sit here all night so I can look at you, but drop the subject, will you? If not you'd be better occupied at home, helping your old man count his gold mines.'

A slight flush tinged her cheeks. Under the tan it was very becoming.

'You're rude, Mr. Preston.'

'You're rich, Miss Freeman. Beautiful and rich. A girl with all that doesn't have a lot of practice at how to behave when refused something.'

She got up from the table. I rose too. The top of her head came up to my nose. If we were dancing I could nuzzle the shining hair. It was a nice thought. It was also very unlikely, if the look on her face was anything to judge by.

'Tell you what,' I said. 'If you're leaving, take this.'

I held out my card, the one that had my private number as well as the office. She took it, held it up to the light where she could read it. Then she stuffed it inside the ridiculous little gold evening purse.

'Tomorrow you may have thought it over,' I suggested. 'You may decide you'd like to talk to me again, this time with the information moving in both directions. I'd be glad to talk to you then.'

She looked at me thoughtfully, seemed about to say something. Then she changed her mind, turned and walked out. To the smooth brown shoulders I said,

'Goodnight, Miss Freeman.' But they didn't hear me.

There was no percentage in sitting down any more. It would be asking too much to expect me to sit and look at an empty chair that had just been occupied by that voluptuous yellow-sheathed body. In any case my glass was empty. I drifted back to the bar and waited while the barkeep did something about it. I had to hand it to Toreno on one count at least. The bottles on view were all filled with the best stuff on the market. Most so-called clubs serve up dishwater with a high alcohol content, but no corners of that kind were being cut in the Broadway Bar. I collected the fresh drink and sampled it. Same as before. Suddenly the crowd quietened down all around. They were looking expectantly at the doorway. Next to me a tall man with a black moustache ran his tongue nervously around his lips. At the entrance to the bar stood a smiling silver-haired man. No tuxedo here. This one was immaculate in full evening dress, tailcoat, stiff white shirt, the whole works. On him it looked good. Holding up his hands for silence he said,

'*Eh bien, mesdames, messieurs*. The Blue Room is now open for your entertainment.'

With that he bowed, turned and walked out. So did everybody else in the place. One man wanted to linger and finish his drink but the woman with him, a grey-haired expensive-looking fifty, tugged at his arm so impatiently that he finally gave up.

That left the man in charge of the bottles and me.

'Does that guy work for the opposition?' I asked.

He smiled.

'Oh no, Mr. Preston. Same business, different department.'

'What's with the French bit, anyhow?'

He shrugged his shoulders. They weren't wide enough to draw attention that way.

'Mr. Toreno says it gives tone. Like the big casinos over there in Europe. Makes for a little colour, Mr. Toreno says.'

It was evident that whatever Mr. Toreno said was O.K. with the bartender.

'Ever been to Vegas?' I queried.

'Mister, I been everywhere. You name a place where they got a licence to peddle booze, I been there.'

He was quite an interesting character. Not that I found that very unusual. Guys who tend bar can be relied on to keep their mouths shut tight on unfavourable subjects. Slip Kerinsky, as he told me his name was, chattered away like a parrot in a South American jungle about the past. On the present he was practically mute. It was as though he'd developed a blind spot. Places he'd worked in before, he described in such detail I could have made up a blueprint. At the Alhambra he was even vague about which room the tables were in. I've had a little experience in asking questions. Slip had quite a little at dodging them. I didn't have any hard feelings about it. A man of his experience wouldn't have been in such good health if he hadn't had a zipper on his vocal chords. He was telling me an involved story about his part-ownership of a sucker-trap in Mexicali a few years earlier, when Al entered the bar.

'Go grab a sandwich, Slip,' he said.

Kerinsky stopped talking right in the middle of a sentence and walked out without a backward glance.

'That guy is all three rolled into one,' I observed.

'Huh?' Al was puzzled. Three what?'

'Three monkeys. You know, hear all, see — '

'Oh yeah, those. Yeah, I heard of those. Slip? He's O.K. Slip minds his own business.'

He stood close to me. His mind seemed far away. Unlike his hands, which hung loosely beside him as though waiting for some signal to come up and take a swing at somebody. It was only his normal stance. Toreno hadn't invested so much in the Alhambra just to have the place turned into a bear-garden by thoughtless employees. If anybody was going to start anything it would not be in the Broadway Bar.

'Any news for me, Al?'

'Oh yeah, sure. Boss says it's O.K. for you to leave now.'

'Why?'

'Huh? How do you mean why?'

As patiently as possible I said,

'What makes it O.K., Al? Why is Toreno showing me the green?'

'Oh that. We found the guys who worked you over. It was like you said. Wiener hired 'em with his own money.'

'Did they say why?' I enquired.

'Sure. A grudge thing, Wiener told 'em. That wouldn't be right, would it?'

'No. I already told your boss I don't know what it was about.'

'Screwy. The whole deal is screwy. But if the boss says O.K., O.K.'

He dug his hand inside his coat and came up with my .38.

'Here,' he tossed it over and I caught it. 'Nothing to keep you here now is there?'

'Nothing,' I assured him.

If it hadn't been for the parked cars outside nobody could have guessed there was a large number of people in the Alhambra. Everything was quiet as I walked back along the terrace. A pleasant breeze had sprung up and I was able to enjoy briefly the experience of what it must feel like to live in a great house like that on such a night. That led me to thinking about Lois Freeman, and indulging in a little fiction as to what might have been if she'd been just a gorgeous dame without all that money.

Nobody bothered me as I pulled out of the car park and headed back down the drive. The gate was already half-open. The character who claimed to be checking membership cards peered in at me, waved a hand in salute, and I was clear of the gate, nose heading for Monkton City.

I was beginning to wish I'd never heard of Moira Chase. I'd been beaten up, slugged from behind, almost hung with a phoney murder rap.

Considering that all I was supposed to be doing was giving the air to an undesirable suitor, things were certainly complicated. Somebody was going to an awful lot of trouble over me, and they weren't through yet. Because from where I sat, the whole bit hinged on the photograph I'd had taken of Kent Shubert. And for all anyone else knew I still had it somewhere. Not that I could understand just what made it so important. Armstrong had told me the piano-player was just a harmless character who liked to put on a jag once in a while. So why all the mystery about the picture? If that was the cause of the excitement. I was as far away from an answer as ever when I hit the outskirts of Monkton.

6

Ten-thirty of a fine summer evening and
Conquest Street was hot as a stove. The
Broadway Bar at the Alhambra had
seemed on the jazzy side an hour before,
but back among the harsh realities of
Conquest I recalled it as a quiet oasis. I
locked the car, crossed my fingers that
most of it would still be there when I got
back, and walked along to the Club
Coastal. I felt the same relief as before
descending the red-carpeted stairway as
the cacophony from the street died
gradually away.

Peggy the hat-check girl had a new
outfit on. Just on the outside that is. The
filling was as before as anybody could
plainly see, and was expected to.

'Well, well,' she greeted. 'The swank
end of town seems to be getting its hooks
into you. Two nights in a row already.'

'I figured if I came regularly I might
just hit the night when you actually fall

out of one of those outfits.'

I pointed to the scraps of material that were scattered sparsely over her frame. She chuckled.

'Why, Mr. Preston, not the sex thing, not from you? I thought you P.I.'s had rooms full of divans, all filled with dames just waiting for you to give 'em a tumble?'

'You know how it is, Peggy,' I said confidentially. 'Man gets to craving for a girl who stands up on her feet once in a while.'

She gave me a crooked grin as I went on inside the club. There were less people than the previous night. The piano-stool was unoccupied. Nobody seemed to want to sit at the bar. Nobody except me that is.

'What'll it be, mister?' The bartender was the same man I'd spoken to last night.

'Make it bourbon and water.'

When he set the drink in front of me, I said,

'Have one yourself.'

'Thanks.'

He poured out another slug from the

same bottle, smacked his lips and took a swallow. I tried my own. It was good stuff.

'Not much action here tonight,' I threw out.

He shook his head.

'Kinda slow. Most of these people won't stay very long. Not unless he shows.'

'Not unless who shows?' I prompted.

'The piano-player, Shubert. He shoulda bin here at eight-thirty.' He was speaking in the complaining tone of somebody who had been at work on time and didn't see why everybody else couldn't do the same.

'Getting late now,' I replied. 'Maybe the man is sick.'

'Pah. Sick. The only sickness that guy ever gets can be cured with raw eggs and pepper. Nope, my guess is he's on a big booze. He's done it before. Last time out it was three whole days before he showed. Then he walks in, sits down and starts playing as though nothing had happened. I tell you, mister, some guys just naturally get born lucky. If I'm thirty minutes late,

Congress holds a special session, but this guy, this piano-player, nobody even mentions it if he lets the job cool for days on end.'

'Tck, tck,' I clicked my tongue sympathetically. 'He's in pretty solid with the boss, huh?'

'You guessed it. Don't ask me why either. He's not even easy to get along with when he is here.'

'That so? What makes it so hard?'

He tipped back some more of the bourbon.

'You can be talking to him see, and maybe he's talking back real friendly. Then all of a sudden he's not with you any more. He starts thinking about something else, and for all he knows you might as well not be there. It's kind of weird.'

'Does anybody try to phone the place he stays at? When he stays off work I mean.'

'Search me,' he heaved his shoulders. 'I don't even know where he sleeps. There's a girl, not much more than a kid, comes in here all the time. If I was making book

I'd give a fair price she could say where he sleeps.' He grinned at me knowingly.

'Like that, huh?' I grinned back, to show the bartender that we were a pretty smart couple of fellows. We knew what time it was. At the same time I was wondering whether he was talking about Ellen Chase. Leaning towards him I said, 'Well, if she's missing tonight as well, could be there's something to your theory.'

He nudged me with his elbow. I love people who do that.

'Right in one. She usually gets here before nine-thirty. But not tonight friend.'

I wondered what I was supposed to do next. I'd been counting on being able to find Shubert at work. Without him there wasn't much more I could do that night. Just one more thing in fact.

'Say, bud, or — talking about girls, reason I came down here tonight was to talk with a little lady. You see, I told her about my — er — stamp collection, and she was interested. She said any time I wanted to show it to her I could find her here.'

'Stamp collection, huh?' he chuckled. 'What will they call it next? What's her name?'

'I don't know her full name. All she said was Fay. She takes the pix in here.'

'That Fay?' He pursed his lips together in a soundless whistle, 'Say she's pretty good, pretty good. What I like about Fay she's got class, you know? Some of 'em now, they're cheap with it. Anybody, any time. Fay's not like that. She has to take a shine to you. You're lucky, mister.'

'Not so lucky,' I pointed out. 'I don't see her.'

'Say that's right. It is getting kind of late for Fay. Maybe some big doings over at the Birds Nest.'

'The Birds Nest? What would she be doing there?' I asked.

'Same as here. Fay doesn't work here, you know.'

'No, I didn't know. Told me she'd be here.'

He nodded impatiently.

'Sure, sure. She comes in, but she works for herself. Got her own deal. She takes the camera outfit to about five joints in turn. Last stop before this is the Birds Nest. If they got some special thing on, big celebration or something, likely she'll be late. Or not make it at all.'

I slid off the stool.

'Well, thanks for the talk,' I said. 'I'll be on my way.'

'Your way being towards the Birds Nest I betcha.' He winked enormously.

I gave him another knowing grin, paid for the drinks and left. The Birds Nest wasn't far to walk. Fay hadn't been in tonight. No, they didn't know where I could reach her, but yes, they knew where she usually worked before the Birds Nest. The name of the place was Murphy's. Fay hadn't been there either but the waiter had a phone number. I scribbled it down, thanked him and got back to the car. I hadn't thought too much about Fay before I found out she wasn't a regular employee of the Club Coastal. That made quite a little difference. Until then, I'd been the man with the photograph, the man you beat up in dark spots. I was the one who mattered, the guy from outside with too long a nose. The point had even

158

been reached where I was far from certain the photograph had any significance. It had meant nothing to Armstrong, and that meant the whole city of San Francisco. But now Fay was beginning to seem important, too. I was the outside man with a photograph, but Fay was the outsider with the negative. So the picture had to mean something. No, not necessarily. I was letting my imagination run away with me. None of it had to mean anything at all. The key was Fay. First I had to find her. If it turned out she had simply decided to have a night on the town, or maybe just sit at home with a head cold, none of it needed to mean anything. One thing I liked about the whole thing dumped in my lap by Moira Chase. It was all so uncomplicated. I didn't think I would be doing very much towards a solution even if I did find Fay. What I needed more than anything was a long conversation with Kent Shubert, but the chances of finding a guy who is on a jag and doesn't want to be found are somewhat slender in Monkton City.

I drove to an all-night garage. I needed

two things, gas and a telephone where I could talk without being overheard. Fay's number was on the Sierra exchange, which covered the section of town in which the garage was situated. There was no reply. I waited a few minutes, tried a second time. Nothing. With the last of my small change I called another number. A man's voice growled.

'Yeah?'

'Let me talk to Charlie,' I said.

'Charlie who?' The tone was guarded.

'You'd be surprised who,' I replied.

'Oh, that one. Who wants him?'

'Tell him it's the guy who prints his own five-dollar bills.'

'Wait a minute.'

He slammed the phone down on some hard surface. The noise it made nearly busted my ear-drum. I could still hear a buzzing when the receiver was picked up again and I heard Charlie Surprise's voice.

'Who's that?'

'Come on now, Charlie, you remember all the way back to this morning don't you? I'm the guy who staked you. You were going to put every book in town down where the red ink is.'

'Oh, it's you.' Charlie didn't exactly sound like a man who just got through breaking the bank.

'Well, did you?'

'Did I what?'

'Did you make a score?'

'A score,' he sounded disgusted. 'How can a guy make a score? Listen, I spread it around, see? Three different tracks. The first four races I'm doing better than six centuries. Are you with me?'

'I'm with you, Charlie.'

'So what happens? On go the bum ones. You know, the real good races. Why those nags were so full of needles, the jocks were getting their legs scratched.'

'And they took you, huh?'

'You could call it that,' he said sadly. 'I am now forty-three bucks to the bad.'

Good. That made Charlie available for almost any kind of activity that promised money. With people like him, real nag-crazy characters, owing money to a book-maker is the one forbidden thing. He would not rest until he had squared the account. Which is why book-makers will always take markers from the Charlie Surprises of this world.

'I could reduce that a little, Charlie, if you'll do something for me,' I offered.

'How little?' he asked cautiously.

'By five dollars.'

'What do I have to do?'

'I've got a telephone number. I want the address that goes with it.'

I could hear his heavy breathing at the other end while he digested that.

'You gotta licence,' he replied finally. 'What's to stop you just asking yourself?'

'I don't want to draw attention to myself in that direction,' I explained patiently.

'Oh.' He thought about that. I could almost hear the cash register ticking away inside his head as he tried to work out how much I could be pushed up on the price. 'Five dollars, you know, that ain't a lot of money. Everything's going up these days. Let's make it ten.'

'Eight,' I said decisively. 'Eight bucks for five minutes' work. Nothing's gone up that far, Charlie. Besides, eight from forty-three leaves exactly thirty-five bucks you'll owe. That's an easier figure to remember.'

'As though I'm liable to forget,' he groaned. 'It's a deal. When do I collect?'

'Drop around the office any time tomorrow. My secretary'll have it for you. This address now. The number is Sierra 00-64109.'

He repeated it slowly.

'One question,' he put in. 'The party we were talking about this morning. This number got anything to do with him? I don't want any trouble with important people.'

'Charlie,' I assured him, 'I can give you my word. Less than two hours ago the man you're talking about swore to me he knew nothing about this particular thing.

'Well, O.K. if you're sure. Where do I reach you?'

I peered in the half-light from the garage neons at the number of the instrument I was holding. I called it over to Charlie Surprise.

'I can't stay around here long,' I warned. 'If you're not back to me in fifteen minutes it's no contract.'

'Can do,' he said briefly. 'Bye.'

I hung up and left the booth with the door standing open. The gas-station attendant was a cheerful kid about nineteen years old.

'Filled her right up, mister. Going far?'

'It depends.'

I handed him a bill and he went inside the brightly-lit office to get my change. The whole front of the office was made up of large glass panels. The cash register was an old-fashioned affair placed close to the door. I could see the youngster open it up, fool around inside, and come up with the change. I could also see the place was deserted except for the two of us. The Company was economising on its payroll by having just one man on duty. There was nothing in the world to prevent me slugging him and cleaning out the cash. Nothing except I didn't have any inclinations that way. Sooner or later somebody would, if for no better reason than the set-up was asking for it. When he came out I stood and chatted with him a while, then the telephone started to jangle from the booth. He started towards it, but I put a hand on his arm.

'It's O.K.,' I said. 'That's for me.'

I went over to the booth and lifted the receiver. The attendant was standing where I'd left him, curiosity written all over his face. I pulled the door shut.

'That you, Charlie?'

'Yeah. Got that address you want.'

He called it out. It was an apartment building two blocks from where I was standing. I checked the telephone number with him one more time, just to be sure we were talking about the right place. I didn't want to go busting in on some private citizen or other in error. Then I thanked him, hung up and went back to the car. The kid was hovering around.

'You a cop or something?' he queried.

I nodded.

'Something. Your security arrangements here don't exactly impress me.'

He was puzzling about that as I rolled away. Perhaps it might make him think just seriously enough to complain to the Company that he was a sitting duck.

There were quite a few lights on in the

building where Fay's apartment was located. No doubt they mostly indicated that the occupants were catching the late movie on television. Folks who make a life-long rule to be in bed by ten every night have had their whole lives altered by the glass box. Before, they wouldn't have walked across the street to see a world title fight from the ringside if it took place at ten-thirty p.m. Nowadays they stay up till all hours to stare at movies that were old before Pearl Harbour.

I wanted the sixth floor. According to the coloured lights over the doors, the elevator seemed to be stuck on eight. I kept on pressing the button in the hope that something would right itself. Nothing did. I began the long tramp up the endless stairway. At the second floor I was beginning to dislike Fay. As I pulled my tired feet over the last tread to the sixth, the dislike had extended to women in general, and most of the rest of the world as well. 609 was the fifth door on the right hand side of the dim-lit corridor. When I reached it I found the door standing open. There were lights on but I could see nobody. I pushed the buzzer. A door closed inside. Then a man appeared.

'Come on in,' he said. 'Who're you?'

I walked in, making sure to check that nobody else was behind the door. The man was in his early twenties, fair-haired, about five feet ten inches tall. His solid frame was covered by a medium-price business suit, together with a quiet shirt and tie. His eyes were hard and bright. These things I noticed second. What struck me right off was the fashion for .38 Police Specials. I had one, he had one. Mine was tucked neatly out of sight beneath my jacket. His was grasped negligently in his left hand, pointing in the general direction of my feet. I got the impression he would be prepared to get it into a more business-like position at very short notice.

'Well,' I said, 'the law. If this is about that parking offence — '

There was a door behind him, undoubtedly the one I'd heard closing while I was out in the hall. Without taking his eyes off me, he rapped on it.

'I got a customer.'

The door opened and in walked Gil Randall. Randall is a sergeant of the Homicide Detail. Forty years old and built like an ox, Randall looks like the screen-writer's dream of a dumb copper, all brawn and no think. He doesn't mind giving that impression, either. People get careless around a cop who doesn't look capable of telling the time of day. They are usually locked up before they realise they've mistaken their man. Randall thinks fast and moves even faster if he has to. With Randall I knew better than to relax.

'Oh, no,' he groaned. 'Not you. You know this joker?'

He turned to the first man and indicated me with his head.

'No, I don't.'

'Well take a look and try to remember him in future. The name is Preston. He calls himself a private investigator. With him that means he gets a free hand to meddle in police business and make himself a nuisance all round.'

Having got that off his chest, he came back to me.

'What're you doing here?'

'I came to see a girl,' I replied.

'What girl?'

'Name of Fay. I don't know the rest of it.'

'All right so you came to see a girl. What about?' Beneath the thick beetling brows his eyes raked my face.

'You have a watch, Randall. What would I come to see a girl about at this hour?'

'Like that, huh?'

He thought about my answer, setting it and me up against the other information he had in his mind. Information I knew nothing about, which put me in the outside position.

'Was she expecting you?' he asked suddenly.

'No, not definitely.'

'When did you see her last?'

'Last night,' I replied.

'Any special time last night? Or just all last night?'

'What is that supposed to mean?' I didn't like the direction Randall was headed.

'It means that your lady friend didn't come home last night. Told the girl in the next apartment. Was she with you?'

I shook my head.

'Uh, uh. Last night I ran into some friends. I thought Rourke might have told you.'

His face was sour.

'Yeah, he told me. So you weren't with her last night. What time did you leave her this evening?'

'This evening? I haven't seen her this evening.'

'You met her at eight-thirty tonight at a bar called Sam's Place. Or do you have so many dames it slipped your mind already?'

Again I gave him a negative.

'Not me, Randall. She may have met somebody. It wasn't me.'

He thought about that for a while, making chewing movements with his jaws.

'So your first approach tonight is to march in here at this hour. Kinda cool, isn't it? Might have been other company here. You coulda phoned.'

'I tried. Thirty minutes ago or there-abouts. There was no answer.'

'So what would be the use in coming?'

'I figured she might be working later than usual. Thought I'd give her thirty minutes to get back, then try calling. If it was still no deal, I'd go home.'

'I see. Well, I got no authority to interfere with the private movements of a citizen. You wanta see her, go ahead. She's inside.'

I didn't want to go into the bedroom. My feet dragged on the rug as I made for the door and opened it. The only light in the room came from a lamp on the bedside table. Fay lay on the bed, her face frozen in an expression of panic-stricken terror. The eyes were open so wide the glassy eyeballs looked as if they might roll out. She wore one nylon stocking, nothing else. Somebody had hacked at her body with a sharp knife. Only a maniac could have produced that insane destruction. Death is never pretty but it can be dignified sometimes. Whoever it was did this to Fay had left her hardly recognisable as human. The bed and floor around were like the walls of a slaughterhouse. Something gripped my stomach and I went green.

'It's in the corner,' said Randall.

I made my way fast in the direction he pointed. Five minutes later, aside from the sour taste in my mouth, I felt well enough to go back into the room where Randall and the other man waited.

'Not very pretty is she?'

Randall wasn't talking tough. He said it softly, in a tone I'd heard before. A tone that meant he'd look forward to finding out who was responsible. I shook my head and searched around for cigarettes.

'Who do you suppose would want to do a thing like that?' he asked me.

'How would I know? You're the guys with the special files on deviates,' I replied.

'Ah, yes, so we are. Did you know, Preston, that we now have a link with every major city on things like this?'

I didn't know why he would bother to tell me that, but so long as he kept talking I was satisfied. I didn't feel like doing much talking on my own account.

'You mentioned something about it a year or two back,' I replied.

'Yeah. Well, it's all buttoned up now. We don't waste any time treating the thing as local business. Even if we knew the name and address of the killer, that still wouldn't mean he couldn't have done the same thing a dozen other places. So we put the whole thing on the wire as fast as we get it. Be surprised at the results. Sometimes half a dozen files get closed with one conviction. If this guy is a pattern killer, we'll know plenty about him by tomorrow night.'

I nodded appreciatively. The cigarette was hitting the spot.

'Do you know why I wanted you to see her, Preston?'

I shook my head.

'Not unless you were hoping I'd be stricken with remorse, as they say, and confess on the spot.'

'Nah.' Randall waved his great hands in front of him. 'I've known you too long. I wanted you to get a good look at what was done to her. Wanted you to get sick in the stomach. It's one thing to talk about a deal like this at headquarters, when you haven't seen it. It's something else again to see it and smell it, until your guts can't take it any more. I wanted you to have that experience.'

'Thanks,' I said bitterly. 'You must hate me good.'

'I don't hate you at all. If you hadn't walked in here tonight your name wouldn't have entered my head. But you did walk in. So you tie in with this Fay. Rourke tells me you did almost the same thing this afternoon. That was a straight-forward shooting, nothing like this. But now suddenly we find a common factor. You. Could be a coincidence. Could be Wednesday's your day for tripping over corpses. Coincidence is something we don't care for at Homicide. So could be there's a connection between these two. Something apart from you. If there is, you've seen what this guy will do. Don't you think he'd be better off the streets?'

His tone was conversational, almost friendly. And he was right. It had been a smart move to let me see Fay just the way she'd been when the killer got through.

The impact had been tremendous. I had a seething hatred of whoever it was did that to her. But it was an anonymous hatred. I might have some names to play with but I didn't know the killer's identity. And if Randall thought I would withhold the name if I had it, even without seeing the body, he was mistaken.

'I can't help you, and that's the truth. I don't know who did this, any more than who killed Little-boy this afternoon. Why does there have to be a connection at all?'

He shrugged.

'Who knows? We have to start some place.'

'You gonna lock this guy up, Sergeant?'

This came from the other plain-clothes man. It was the first thing he'd uttered for about twenty minutes. Randall looked at him pityingly.

'Oh, sure. Just how many charges did you have in mind?'

The other was taken aback.

'Why I, er, just on suspicion, I guess.'

'Suspicion, huh? Suspicion of what? The guy didn't kill that girl.'

The fair-haired man was new to me.

That, coupled with Randall's attitude towards him, told me he was new to the Detective Division as well. He decided to bluster on with it.

'How do we know that, Sergeant? Nobody asked him where he's been all night.'

'You're not going to like this,' I told him. 'I've been trying to find Fay.'

There was no change of expression in the stare.

'Trying where?'

I told him where. I gave him a complete run-down on the places I'd been, who I talked with, times and so on. When I was through, Randall nodded, turned back to his assistant.

'Satisfied?'

'No. He tells us all this. How do we know it checks? How do we know he won't walk straight out of here and catch a night-flight to Hong Kong or some place?'

Randall let out a short whoosh of breath between his teeth. He does that when he has resigned himself to something he doesn't like. In this case, explaining to the new boy about me.

'Two questions there. First off, how do we know it checks? I'll tell you how, because he says so. Because I've checked him out on fifty yarns like that in the past, and they always check.' He held up a hand as the other man started to speak, 'Wait. We'll still follow it through. Thoroughly. But it'll check. Then I believe there was something about Preston making a fast exit. That won't happen. To my mind anybody who calls himself a private investigator is an undesirable citizen. Including Preston. He's been getting in my hair for years one way and another. But he doesn't cut up dames with butcher's knives.'

There was a flat finality in the way he spoke the last sentence. The lecture was over. The new man was not invited to ask any more questions.

'Thanks, Randall,' I said. 'Can I use you as a reference?'

'Don't be smart,' he growled. 'I know I oughtn't to let you go. The right thing for me to do is take you down-town and put a few friendly questions to you. In the basement. You have to know something about all this.'

It was the cue for the rookie to come back into the game.

'So why don't we, Sergeant? Take him down, I mean?'

'Because, sonny, I'm the officer in charge here. I'm at the top of the sergeants' list, did you know that? A year, more or less, I get a gold badge. Lieutenant Rourke now, he's had a gold badge twelve years already. And Lieutenant Rourke decided to let this man go free this afternoon on a similar charge. So the rules say, if I want to knock him off for anything, I have to consult the senior officer first. Get it?'

'Sure, but the lieutenant's only at home. We could call him up — '

'Call him up? You don't listen very good, do you? The lieutenant is in bed. He didn't get to bed last night at all. When he let Preston go this afternoon he had reasons. They're usually pretty good reasons. Preston isn't gonna blow town, tonight or any night. So if anybody wants to wake up the lieutenant in the middle of the night to ask if it's O.K. to question somebody who can be questioned just as easily in the morning, it's not gonna be me. Am I getting through to you yet?'

His assistant subsided.

'You heard what I said, Preston. Reason you're walking out of here is not because I'm through with you. Better get, before I let this wetpants talk me into something foolish. Be at headquarters tomorrow morning. Early.'

There are times to argue, and times when anything you say is liable to be wrong. I made for the door and got away before he changed his mind. As I headed home I was trying to tell myself that what had happened to Fay was nothing to do with the other things. Nothing to do with Shubert and Ellen Chase, with Moira or Toreno. Or Little-boy Wiener, whose body would be stiffening now in its ice-cold compartment at the morgue. And yet I knew that everything tied in. It was obvious from where I sat that the man who killed Fay had deliberately set out to make it look like the work of a psychopath. I didn't believe he — or she

— was crazy for a minute. Just smart. Fiendishly, diabolically smart. I shuddered at the brief memory of Fay's body lying across the bed. What kind of a mind could anybody have that would even suggest such a way to throw off suspicion? I was certain of something else too. Fay had been killed because she had the negative of a certain photograph of which I had the only print. And if I was right about that, I knew that whoever had done that to Fay had been the one who hired Little-boy Wiener to work me over. The only one who could possibly be that concerned had to be the man whose picture it was, Kent Shubert. And Shubert was missing from the Club Coastal. If it was him putting up the death rate he had to know I still possessed a print of the picture. And that meant he would have to come after it himself.

I drove into the basement garage of my apartment building, switched off the motor and killed the lights. Then I got out of the car and walked up the concrete slope at the side of the building, the same way I'd taken the night before when

Wiener and company jumped me. I didn't know I was all tensed up until I reached the top. Then I felt a sudden relaxing all over, and realised I'd been waiting for somebody to try the same thing. I headed for the main entrance to the building.

7

It was eight-thirty on a fine Thursday morning and as I sat brooding over a cup of coffee I was trying to convince myself it was great to be alive on such a day. The thought kept intruding that maybe lucky would be a more appropriate word. The night had been restless. I'm not an unusually nervous type, but I seemed to have something that was wanted by somebody else. Fay had had something too, and I'd seen what the somebody did to her. Thanks to Randall. So I spent a good part of the night imagining I could hear someone creeping about the place. Someone with a butcher's knife in his hand. It was a relief when the first faint cracks of light appeared through the windows. Finally I did catch a couple of hours and now I sat hunched across a table, the aromatic steam from the coffee curling up into my face from the cup that was cradled between my hands.

The door-buzzer sounded suddenly. I took no notice, hoping the caller would go away. No dice. This time it was pushed and released intermittently, as though somebody was practising the Morse code.

'All right, all right,' I shouted, then trailed my sleepy way across to the door. I thumbed back the lock and opened up. Moira Chase stood outside. It didn't look as though she'd been getting too much sleep either.

'Mr. Preston, Ellen's disappeared.'

Her voice was agitated. The words seemed to blurb themselves out. She stood there transferring her purse continually from one hand to the other.

'Take it easy,' I told her. 'Come inside.'

She stepped in past me, eyes widening at sight of the .38 held in the hand which had been hidden by the door. I stuck it in my pocket and motioned her towards a chair. She sat down obediently, but at once leapt to her feet and began roaming around, like a cat looking for the exit.

'All right, Mrs. Chase. Better tell me the story,' I said. 'By the way, would you like some coffee?'

She shook her head. Her hair hadn't had much attention today, but tumbled as it was, it only looked like one of those 'natural' hair-styles that cost so much money. This was as I'd imagined she'd look without the bun.

'No, thanks. She's gone. Really gone. I searched the whole town. It is just as though she dropped into the sea — '

Realising the implication of that, she stopped the flow of words, and bit her lower lip with the strong even teeth.

'I mean — ' she began.

'I know what you mean, Mrs. Chase.' I tried to be gentle with her. 'Now look. You've got something to tell me. I want to hear it all, and that will take a few minutes anyway. If the world is going to come to an end we'd better talk about it seriously. Those few minutes are not going to make any material difference. Why not sit down? Please.'

Moira nodded, went back to her chair and sat stiffly on the edge.

'Have you had any breakfast?' I queried.

Again the brown hair waved from side to side.

'You're all in,' I said. 'We'll talk after you've had some coffee.'

She didn't even try to argue. While I fussed around finding another cup, she sat quite still, not saying a word, just staring out of the window. I put the coffee down beside her. She didn't seem to notice.

'Drink it,' I commanded. 'Here.'

Lifting her hand I put the cup in it. She looked at me, dark rings beneath the troubled eyes. Then she sipped at the cup, swallowed, and made a face.

'No sugar,' she protested.

I produced sugar. She stirred some in to the steaming liquid, tried again.

'Wonderful,' she admitted.

By the time she had drunk half the cup I noticed she was relaxing slightly, sitting further back in the chair, looking more comfortable.

She took a cigarette from the pack I extended, banged the tip once on the arm of the chair, lit it and swallowed smoke.

'Thank you.'

'Sorry I haven't any Turkish,' I apologised. 'If I thought you might get to be a regular visitor I'd do something about it.'

'This is fine.'

Surprising what a cup of coffee and a cigarette will do for people. I've seen guys who haven't been near a bed in three days getting ready to tramp ten miles through mud after a break of that kind. Somebody with brains is going to bottle whatever it is that does the trick some day. That guy will be onto a fast million.

'Let's try it now,' I suggested. 'Start at the beginning. When did you see Ellen last?'

'Yesterday afternoon. After you left the house she came back inside. You seemed to make quite an impression on her. She wanted to know who you were, all about you.'

'Did you tell her?'

'Not then. She thought you were — a — er,'

'A friend of yours?' I suggested. 'A man friend?'

'Yes.' She looked down at the floor, seeming almost embarrassed. 'You know how these teenagers can't understand a man and a woman having any possible subject to discuss except that one.'

'I know. Sometimes I think the teenagers have a point of view.'

She smiled slightly, but it was quickly gone.

'It was after lunch that the trouble started. I went for a walk outside, Ellen told me she had a few telephone calls to make, and I wasn't going to stay in the house while she held those interminable discussions about the latest jazz recordings. When I got back to the house she was waiting for me. I've never seen her quite that angry before. She told me what she'd been doing. She'd called up every M. Preston in the book until she found out which one was you.'

'Ah,' I nodded. 'My secretary told me a woman phoned yesterday afternoon. Didn't ask for me, just wanted to know if I was the right Preston. That must have been Ellen.'

In a way I was glad. At the back of my mind had been a nagging suspicion that it might possibly have been Fay, and if I'd been able to talk to her she might not be dead now. I felt relieved on that score at least.

'That was Ellen,' agreed Moira. 'She guessed immediately it would have some connection with herself and this man Shubert. She took me so much by surprise, that I'm afraid I said more than I intended.'

'You told her about our business?'

'Yes. I wouldn't have done normally. I'm not a hysterical woman, but if you'd seen the mad rage Ellen was in — . It took me completely unawares. I wasn't ready for her.'

'Understandable,' I soothed. 'What happened then?'

'She raged on for quite a while. Mr. Preston, I wouldn't have thought it possible to live in the same house with somebody for years, and yet not realise them to be capable of making a scene like that. I — I guess we both got worked up.' Her face was troubled at the memory of the quarrel with her stepdaughter. 'Finally she went to her room. I thought she'd probably sulk for a few hours, then we could talk about it sensibly. But in the early evening she suddenly walked back in complete with a packed bag. She was leaving, she told me.

'To go to Shubert?'

'She didn't actually say that. Just that she was leaving and she wouldn't be coming back. In a few months time she'd inherit her father's money. There'd be plenty of people who'd lend her enough to pay hotel expenses until her birthday.'

'Did you try to stop her, Mrs. Chase?'

'Not physically. I begged her not to go. She wouldn't discuss it with me. She said I'd had every opportunity in our earlier conversation to say anything I had to say. Short of tying her to a chair I didn't see there was much I could do to stop her.'

Which was true enough.

'Has she a car of her own?'

'She has a red M.G. It's one thing that gives her a lot of pleasure. She frequently goes out and drives two or three hundred miles just for fun.'

'Pretty fast for a girl of seventeen, isn't it? I mean considering that she lives a fairly quiet life in other directions.'

'That's exactly why I let her have it.

She's an expert driver, quite one of the best I've seen. I've never had to worry about that, at least.'

'All right. So she threw the bag in the car and took off. Then what?'

'I didn't worry too much at first. I was certain she'd head for a friend's home, and the parents would waste no time letting me know where she was. Then I called up one or two likely places, without success. Gradually I became more concerned. I phoned Bart Lytton. He took it quite seriously from the first. Told me to bring a good photograph of Ellen to his home at once. When I got there he had three men waiting for me. They were from a big agency, Fording's would it be?'

'Fordhams,' I corrected. 'They're nation-wide. Very reliable people and all that. I'd hate to seem difficult at a time like this, but I do have kind of an interest in this. Why not bring me in? As well as Fordham's I mean. I know they've got the big organisation. I'm not knocking them, they're a first-class outfit with more resources than I'll ever have. But I do have an interest.'

My interest right then being primarily to find out just why I was excluded. Moira nodded vigorously.

'Oh yes, exactly what Mr. Lytton said. But he'd been trying to call you and got no answer. I tried myself from his house, twice.'

'What time would that be?'

'Oh, eight-thirty, and again probably an hour later.'

Check. I'd been on my way to the Alhambra. And earlier, when I'd tried to contact Moira, she'd been on her way to Lytton's house.

'I was out then,' I agreed. 'So these boys went on a tour of the hotels and so forth, looking for Ellen. What did you do meantime?'

'I went home. We arranged that they would report there if they had any news. I felt I had to be home in case Ellen changed her mind, or had an accident or anything.'

'Of course. You put these boys onto the Club Coastal, naturally? And the piano-player?'

'Yes. I didn't tell them anything too

personal. Just said he was a friend of hers and she often went to hear him play.'

'Well, she didn't get to hear him last night. He didn't show at the club, and Ellen hadn't been around up to the time I left there.'

Moira jerked her head in agreement.

'I know. When I heard that was when I began to get frightened. Mr. Preston, I give you my word, if I find out in ten minutes time that Ellen and this man Shubert are married, I won't care. Just as long as I know she's safe. But these men have covered the whole town. They're experts, if they say she's not here I have to believe them. But she hasn't been home all night. I'm frightened. Deep down frightened so I don't want to talk about it. I'm scared to examine what I'm thinking too closely. I might go mad.'

The agitation was back. Her breasts were rising and falling with suppressed emotion and her breathing was hard.

'Get hold of yourself,' I said harshly. 'I've got enough trouble here without some leaky dame splashing up the furniture.'

It was as though somebody had flung a bucket of ice water in her face.

She caught her breath sharply, rose and rushed at me.

'I'll kill you, I'll kill you,' she shouted, raking at me with her nails. I stepped back quickly and brought my hand round against her cheek. She stopped cold. The white marks made by my hand showed stark against the tan. Moira stood there swallowing great gulps of air. We looked at each other. Slowly she raised a hand to her face and stroked gently at the cheek I'd struck. When she spoke her voice was controlled normally.

'I'm sorry. I'm not much help am I?'

'I'm sorry, too. Later, you can take a free swing at me. Right now we have a lot to do.'

'Do?' She was puzzled. 'What can we do that's going to be of any value? You told me yourself you couldn't hope to compete with Fordhams.'

I wagged my head in a negative.

'I didn't say that at all. I said they had more resources that's all. There are things I know that they don't. And that you don't.'

193

A faint sparkle appeared momentarily in the dark eyes.

'You mean you have some idea where she might be?'

'I'm not going to raise your hopes by saying that. But there are a few things to be done arising out of that harmless little enquiry you wanted me to make. And you can help.'

'Anything,' she said eagerly. 'Anything at all. What do you want me to do?'

'First of all, answer a question. When Lytton's men reported that Shubert was missing from the Club Coastal, did you think to ask Toreno if he knew where you could look for him?'

She nodded.

'Oh, yes, that was the first thing I thought of doing.' Her tone was bitter. 'My good friend Vic Toreno was rude to me. Very rude. He said he wasn't Shubert's keeper, and what did I mean asking him. He didn't keep tabs on every piano-player on the West Coast, and as for Ellen she'd probably found herself a truck-driver for a few nights. These society kids were always doing something of the kind. From what he'd seen of Ellen she looked the same as the rest.'

I didn't know quite what to say to that. Even for Toreno, it was a pretty raw reply to a supposed girl-friend who was obviously at her wits end with worry. Or on the other hand, some people might see it differently. Might think that what was upsetting Moira Chase was not so much the disappearance of her stepdaughter as the probable break-up with her boy-friend, Toreno. That's what some people might think. Nasty suspicious-minded people. People like me.

'So I take it you're not so, shall we say friendly towards Vittorio right now?'

'I never want to see him again.' She meant it.

'That's good. How you feel I mean. Not the bit about not seeing him. It may be necessary.'

'May I ask why?'

'Look, Mrs. Chase, you're not a child, so I'm not going to treat you like one. Toreno is a hoodlum. You know it as well as I do. Up till now it hasn't bothered you, because it hasn't touched you. Well, that's O.K. with me, I'm not a preacher.'

'I knew he must have more in his past than just gambling. He's pushed his way up from the streets, and I know that isn't too easy. But I thought it was all behind him. He's got the Alhambra, and the only illegal thing there is the gambling. You won't find one person in three in this state who regards that as a real crime.' She looked at me with defiance. 'All right if you want to know what I thought, I thought he was a crook who'd made some money and now regarded himself as almost semi-retired.'

'Did you love him?' I asked quietly.

'Love,' she curled her lip at the word. 'What would I know about love? All I ever seemed to attract were propositions before I met F. Harper Chase. Compared to what had gone before, his offer was quite straightforward and much more profitable. So I let an old man buy me in return for comfort and security. You asked me about love, Mr. Preston. I don't know. But Vic Toreno was an all-male animal that I liked to be near. Would that cover it?'

'It might,' I replied. 'Was that how he felt, too?'

'Yesterday I would have said yes. Today, I'm not so sure. Oh, don't get the wrong impression. This isn't a case of either one of us being mad about the other. But we had something I thought was mutually satisfactory.'

I shifted in the chair to a position where I wouldn't find Moira's slim legs in the direct line of vision all the time.

'If you don't like any of my questions, just tell me to go to hell,' I said. 'But remember it's you I'm asking them for.'

'Go ahead, Mr. Preston. What can there be left that you don't know about me?'

'It's not you I'm most interested in at the moment. It's Toreno. Tell me, what was his relationship with Ellen?'

Some of her informality disappeared.

'With Ellen? What precisely does that mean?'

'Not what you're obviously thinking. I mean did he joke with her as a man his age might, or did he treat her as an equal, or what?'

'Oh,' there was a slight thaw, 'they only met a few times. I'd say he teased her a little about some of her fads, but on the whole they were friendly. Yes, more as equals I'd say.'

'Uh, huh. How long had you known Toreno before he started including Shubert in the deal?'

Her forehead screwed up as she concentrated.

'A fortnight. Might have been three weeks. I don't remember exactly.' Then, 'Look here, you're not suggesting Vic brought that man along just for the purpose of getting him involved with Ellen? Why, that's ridiculous.'

I sighed. We hadn't even got to the hard part yet.

'Perhaps. You told me yesterday Toreno brought Shubert to your house. How did he come to do that?'

She thought about it for a moment, then, 'Vic is very enthusiastic about jazz pianists. I probably told you that?'

I inclined my head.

'He mentioned Shubert several times to me. Promised to get him out to the

Alhambra one evening especially for my benefit. Then he did. I was flattered that he should go to that trouble.'

'Naturally. Did Ellen go with you to the Alhambra that night?'

'No. It was a surprise for me. Vic does things like that. Ellen was envious when I told her about it.'

'Why?'

'Because she wanted to hear him too. She'd been down to the Club Coastal on several occasions with her friends. It would have been a great triumph for her to be able to tell them she'd been entertained by Shubert privately.'

Now we were coming to the part Moira wasn't going to like.

'So Toreno suggested that he make it up to her by bringing Shubert to the house for a drink one evening?'

'Yes, something like that.' Her face showed surprise. 'I forget the details but that's close enough. What are you driving at, Mr. Preston?'

I cleared my throat.

'Mrs. Chase, I'm going to go through a few facts with you. They're all things you already know, so it may seem pointless at first. Bear with me. What I'm trying to do is re-assemble things in a new order. When I get through the picture may look a whole lot different to you.'

She smiled uncertainly.

'I haven't the remotest idea what you're talking about, but I suppose I'm willing to try it. Why won't I like facts that I already know and accept?'

'That will be for you to judge,' I told her. 'Oh, and one condition. Please don't interrupt. You'll lose the sequence.'

She gave me a curious look, nodded and settled back in the chair.

'Go ahead.'

'We'll start a few months back. We find two women living in a house in Monkton City. One is beautiful.

She flushed with pleasure. I bowed slightly from the chair.

'Beautiful, the right side of thirty, moderately wealthy. The other is a good-looking teenager, growing up into a knockout. In a few months time the teenager stands to inherit not less than one-fifth of a million dollars. A very large sum of money, even in these times.'

While I was still talking I went over to the table and emptied the last dregs of cold coffee into my cup.

'A gambler arrives in town. Somehow he has managed to acquire the use of a very exclusive property. He turns it into a gambling casino. For reasons of his own he also buys a trap on Conquest Street. Conquest is quite a car-ride from Millions Mile. The Club Coastal doesn't seem to jell with the Alhambra, but the gambler buys just the same. Into the Club Coastal he introduces a piano-player. Not just any old key-thumper, but a stylist, a musician with something to offer. Why put a man of that talent into a joint like the Coastal?'

She nodded vigorously.

'Exactly. Why Shubert could have made a fortune on television or — '

Her voice tailed away when she saw the look on my face.

'No interruptions, please. Anyway I didn't put the question with any hope of getting an answer. I still don't know what it is. However, that's the set-up. Pretty soon people are going along to listen to the music. All kinds of people. Poor people, rich people. We'll forget about the poor right now, concentrate on the rich. Especially girls. One of the girls is our teenager. She attends with a number of others. Plenty of them have money, or will come into money. The gambler sets about looking into this group, at least the girl members. Mostly they come from homes with the regulation number of parents. One or two cases where divorce has come into the picture, but they are disqualified on other grounds. Perhaps Mama is a lush, or perhaps she is fat and forty and knows she would be unlikely to attract a man like the gambler just on her physical merits.'

From my new position by the table I squinted at Moira. She was pale now. There was no attempt at interruption.

'These women had to be disqualified, as I say. They would imagine the gambler was after their money and be suspicious of him, and any friend he brought along. They would be wrong in the first instance. The gambler would not be interested in their money at all, or certainly only as a secondary consideration. So he keeps on looking. Finally he comes to our teenager. No father, no mother. Instead a stepmother. She's young and beautiful. Any man would be a fool not to try for her, money or not. The gambler tries.'

Before she had an opportunity to say anything I hurried on.

'He tries, and he's a man who has a way with women. The stepmother is interested. A little intrigued too at being associated with an underworld character. Oh,' I waved a hand as she opened her mouth, 'it's all happened before. The gambler is now ready to bring in his friend the piano-player. Teenager is suitably impressed. Pretty soon we have two couples. The gambler's idea is to let things roll along for another few months, then the teenager comes into her inheritance. The piano-player marries two hundred thousand dollars, and with any luck at all the stepmother will not even realise she's been hooked. If she does, that won't matter either once the ceremony is over.'

I decided to have a break in the story at that point. Moira had scarcely been listening for the last few sentences anyway. She'd been able to leap ahead once I got about two-thirds of the way through. Silence hung thick in the room as I finished talking. It was a relief when Moira finally spoke.

'Well, well.' Her voice was small. I imagined she was feeling that way all over. 'So Moira Chase, hard-boiled Moira Chase, has been taken to the cleaners.'

That expression, I noted, was one which had undoubtedly been in cold storage since the days before she became Mrs. F. Harper Chase.

'Try not to feel too badly about it. Even supposing I'm right, I doubt whether anybody ever had such a pleasant part to play as Toreno did.'

She managed a tiny smile. Very tiny. I knew how she must be feeling. In my curious business I've often had to disillusion wealthy women about their boy-friends, but none of them had ever possessed the other attractions Moira Chase had. For her it was as natural for men to be interested in her as it was for the sun to come up in the morning. Anyway, having given the medicine straight, I could now come across with the sugar coating.

'Now we get a little more up-to-date with the story. So far everything has been working out exactly the way Toreno figured. What he hadn't bargained for was your genuine love for your stepdaughter. He undoubtedly thought, and you'll forgive my saying this, what most outsiders would think. Attractive girl marries elderly man for his money. Elderly man dies, so there's no longer any necessity for his widow to pretend any interest in her stepdaughter. Only yours wasn't pretence. You intended to go right on watching out for Ellen until she was old enough to take care of herself.'

'Why, of course,' she agreed. 'That was why I came to you.'

'I know. And that's what started all this trouble. As soon as I started to show some interest in Kent Shubert the sky fell in.'

She looked at me unhappily.

'And now Ellen's gone. That's the latest and most horrible thing of all.'

'I won't necessarily agree with that until I know where she is. Do you feel up to answering one or two more questions?'

'I suppose so,' she said wearily. 'We don't seem to be getting very far, but if you think it might help — '

'I think so. First, if Ellen gets married before the age of eighteen, or if anything should happen to her, what happens to the two hundred thousand dollars?'

Below her ears a dull red tinge appeared.

'I see what you're driving at, but you're wrong. In either case the whole of Ellen's interest in the estate is revoked. The money then goes to the party funds.'

'The Senator's party?'

'Yes.'

'Thank you. I had to ask. With that kind of money involved, there might have been some other relative who stood to inherit. Such a person would probably have been able to throw a little light on recent events.'

'Sorry to disappoint you,' she observed.

'Not at all. It's at least an avenue of enquiry we can save time exploring. Something else I want to know. Did Toreno ever confide in you as to exactly how he managed to acquire the lease of the Alhambra?'

'No, he didn't. I was curious about that. I've lived around here long enough to know about the little difficulties that are put in the way of undesirables who try to move into the Mile. I often asked him, but he would only grin and say he had his methods, or something of the kind.'

'I see. Did you ever hear of a girl named Lois Freeman?'

Her mouth moved into an expression of distaste.

'Yes, I've talked to her once or twice.'

'But you don't like her very much,' I prompted.

'No. She made scenes at the club sometimes. The trouble is she's insanely in love with Vic. Hangs around wherever he is, always pestering at him.'

'So probably she hasn't gone out of her way to be pleasant to you. You being a woman who's been having more success with Toreno.'

'Oh, no, she's never been rude to me. What makes me dislike her is the way she chases after him. She's attractive enough not to need to do that. I don't imagine with her looks and money she would have any difficulty in acquiring male company. That's what used to make me so angry, watching her following Vic around like some lapdog. I can't stand to see a woman humble herself that way. It lets down the whole sex.'

I thought about that for a few moments.

'You obviously know that Lois is the daughter of Marsland Freeman II?' I said. 'Did you also know that the Alhambra was Marsland Freeman's property?'

'Why, no,' she was surprised. 'Then that would explain how Vic got hold of it. Lois must have talked her father into it.'

'Could be.' It was a possibility and only that. By no means the foregone conclusion that Moira seemed to think. A man who builds a forty-seven million dollar empire largely by his own efforts, is not the kind to be buffaloed by anybody, including his own daughter. But it was a possibility. 'If Lois was such a nuisance to our friend Toreno, why didn't he stop her coming to the club? I seem to remember it isn't an easy place to get in if they don't want you.'

'I asked him that too. He told me it was easier said than done. If he really did anything to offend a man as important as Mr. Freeman he'd be out of business in a week. And Mr. Preston,' her eyes were serious, 'I've seen that kind of thing too often to doubt it.'

'Me too. One thing puzzled me, though. A woman with a fixation like that being polite to the opposition. It doesn't figure.'

'That's what I used to think. When I put it to Vic, he told me that after talking with me quite civilly she would go outside and call him on the private phone. She would say things about me that he wouldn't repeat. Horrible things, things that showed a diseased mind.'

I looked at my watch. Florence Digby would have the office open by now.

'We ought to get started,' I announced. 'We've got a busy day ahead.'

She rose from the chair, smoothing down her clothes.

'You've helped me to get a better grip on myself, talking sensibly like this. Thank you.'

'I couldn't have done anything if you hadn't been a moderately tough character already,' I grinned.

'Before we go, I'd like to ask a question myself. If you're right in your analysis, and I've a nasty suspicion you are, why should Vic Toreno go to all that trouble to get Shubert married to a lot of money?' Then before I could reply, 'Incidentally, where are we going anyway?'

'That's two questions,' I pointed out. 'Answer to the first one, I don't know. There should be some history on Toreno in this morning's mail at my office. That may give us a lead. Answer to question two. Where we're going is to that same office.'

She stood in front of a mirror and ran a comb through her hair. The sun caught the rich sheen of it. Absent-mindedly I thought how much I preferred it without the bun. She turned from the mirror and smiled. She was standing very close.

'Really? Thank you.'

I was off guard.

'Huh? For what?'

'You said you liked it better without the bun. I do too.'

So now I was taking to thinking out loud. Next thing was dual conversation in my lonely room. After that it was a short step to the quiet hospital where nothing sharp is on view. Brusquely I said,

'Let's get going.'

Moira had her own car parked in front of the building. It was this year's Cadillac in cream and blue. When Moira slid behind the wheel anybody could see the designer had had her in mind from the first. She purred easily into town looking like one million dollars American. I kept a respectful distance behind, looking and feeling like the man who carries the bags.

If I'd been thinking faster I'd have had sense enough to call Florence Digby up and tell her I'd asked Moira to meet me at the office. As it was we arrived together a little after nine-thirty in the morning. Miss Digby hasn't worked for a private investigator all this time without acquiring some technique in deductive reasoning. Her eyebrows, customarily disapproving, contrived to edge a quarter of an inch higher.

'Morning, Miss Digby,' I was jovial. 'Mrs. Chase was just on her way to see me. Met in the lobby.'

Moira smiled at her. Any effect that may have had was not noticeable.

'I've dealt with the mail, Mr. Preston. There's a large envelope from San Francisco on your desk.'

'Thank you. Come on in, Mrs. Chase.'

I ushered Moira into my room, closed the door and helped her get seated.

'You were quick with an explanation, just now,' Moira was amused. 'Do I gather Miss Digby might be thinking dark thoughts about you and I?'

I was busy ripping open the white envelope from Armstrong Investigations.

'Miss Digby,' I remarked, 'has a very low opinion of me in many departments. Especially my morals. I don't know where she gets these ideas.'

Moira tut-tutted in mock sympathy.

'And you such a quiet-living man, too.'

We grinned. Grinning at a female like Moira Chase is nice work. Especially when she grins in return. I spread out the papers on the desk. There was a hand-written note from Joe Armstrong telling me what a lot of hard work his staff had put in to get me the enclosed information in time. I knew Joe of old. This was the softening up for the large bill that would follow a few days later. Some of the stuff enclosed was known to me, much of the rest was of no particular significance to the present investigation. But the rap sheet, the record of involvement with the law, was a lulu.

CONFIDENTIAL REPORT

Subject: (Surname) TORENO (first names) VITTORIO ALBERTO (VIC) b. New York 1921.

Arrested May 16, 1933, Robbery. Sentence: Work farm: two years.

Arrested November 4, 1935, Robbery.

Sentence: Boy's reformatory: three years.

Arrested September 10, 1939, Armed Robbery. Case dismissed: Lack of evidence.

Arrested January 8, 1942, Grand Larceny. Acquitted: Names of two jurors later deleted.

Held for questioning, March 6, 1944. Suspicion of Murder of George (Lucky) Rafini — Released.

Arrested December 16, 1945, Sullivan Law State withdrew owing to disappearance of material witness.

Arrested June 25, 1948, Extortion. Sentence: One to five (served two years in Ossining).

And there was more, lots more. Pinned to the record were clippings of various newspaper shots of the many cases in which Toreno had taken up space. I was so intent on my reading that I clean forgot Moira Chase was present. Since the conviction in 1948 Toreno had been hauled in for questioning a dozen times, and for as many types of offence, but the two-year spell up the river had evidently bred caution in our hero, and he had not been a guest of the State of New York since. The move to California had been in 1957, and by that time it was clear from reading between the lines, Toreno now moved in the upper echelons. He no longer needed to do any dirty work with his own hands. For that he used others, which costs money. Money it seemed was a problem of the past to Vittorio (Vic) Toreno. There were two other items that rated reading for a second time. One was a clipping from the gossip column of a New York daily. The dateline read April 10, 1956.

. . . and what is this I hear? Man-about-town Vic Toreno hooked at last by a lady named Elizabeth. And I do mean a real, razz-ma-tazz lady, people. Not from this lil ole village, that I do know, but they say the fair one is dripping with uranium. Vic wouldn't tell me what stripper Lola Van Gough had to say to the news, and anyhow this newspaper does not print words of that kind . . .

At the back of the clipping was a note written by one of Armstrong's assistants.

' — There is evidence that Toreno was married early in 1956 to a woman reputed to be of good social background. The ceremony must have been held by some upstate justice of the peace who did not realise whom he was marrying. The wife seems to have been an alcoholic or worse. Her name was Elizabeth, age approximately twenty-two at the time of marriage. According to reports she was beautiful, self-willed and extremely wealthy in her own right. She was believed to have left her husband shortly before he moved to California in May, 1957. For details of background information leading to Toreno's decision to leave New York, see attachment eleven.'

Attachment eleven was a four-column spread in a Sunday paper, dateline March 22, 1957.

SEX-KILLER DIES IN POLICE BATTLE

At one o'clock this morning GIO-VANNI TORENO, musician, age 25, died in a gun-battle with police officers. Toreno was wanted for questioning in connection with the recent sex-slayings which have terrorised 42nd Street. Three show-girls are known to have died by the same hand, the most recent being Eleanor (Cuddles) Candy, 19, whose headless torso was recovered from the East River on Tuesday of this week. Following up reliable information that Toreno was the maniac responsible, police stopped him for questioning as he was leaving a club owned by his brother Vittorio. Toreno broke away and in the running gun-fight which followed, two police officers were wounded, one seriously. Toreno was trapped from both ends while attempting to cross the Brooklyn Bridge. As officers closed in he tried to climb one of the girders at the side of the bridge. Officer Morando shot him as he clung there, and the body fell into the river. Dragging for the body is now in progress. Citizens of Broadway will heave a sigh of relief today, when they hear of — '

And so forth. There were details of the crimes committed by the late and obviously unlamented Giovanni Toreno. The names of the victims were unfamiliar but the way in which the murders were committed was not. Cuddles Candy and the rest had died in an identical manner to Fay. It struck me that I still didn't even know her last name. I don't mind a little coincidence now and then but this was more than I could stomach. There were two possibilities only so far as I could guess. Either the police had killed the wrong man when they gunned Giovanni Toreno off the Brooklyn Bridge, or he had somehow managed to survive the fall. I forced myself to wade through every word of the four columns in an endeavour to find something that might help. It was strictly fill-up material for the most part. There was a sooty picture of Giovanni, a slim cocky-looking boy with dark curly hair. The picture must have been lifted off an old shot and it hadn't benefited by reproduction. It could have been anybody, me, you the guy in the next chair in the barber shop. Then right at the foot of the page, beneath an ad for girdles, I found something. Smudgy black type announced:

FOUR AM
(See this page)

IDENTIFY KILLER CORPSE

Battered body recovered from river identified as Giovanni Toreno. Brother Vittorio wept as Giovanni's business associate Samuel Wiener (31) confirmed identification.

Now we were getting warmer. If Vic Toreno and Little-boy had been the only two to identify Giovanni's body — and that would need checking — the field was wide open. As to whether Giovanni was still alive or not I didn't know. What I did know was that the New York killer of years before was still alive, and setting up in practice again. I also knew beyond any doubt that Vic Toreno was either the killer, or he knew who was and probably where to find him.

'May I have one, too?'

Moira's voice suddenly brought me back to the present. I'd taken out my pack of Old Favourites and lit one for myself without passing them around.

'Of course. I'm sorry.'

'Not at all. I hardly dared to ask, you were so wrapped up with your reading.'

She indicated the stuff on my desk.

'Plenty to think about in here,' I confirmed. 'I don't want to rub in anything, but as you're not feeling so friendly towards Toreno at the moment, you may like to read this little biography of your harmless gambler.'

I passed over the list of Toreno's crimes and the cutting about his marriage. The spread about brother Giovanni I kept back. Moira Chase was nobody's fool. She would soon be able to make two and two come to four if I gave her the clipping. For her, four would equal Kent Shubert, and Shubert was possibly to be found in the same place as Ellen, wherever that might be. Moira had as much to worry about as she could reasonably be expected to carry, without adding more.

Her face was expressionless as she checked Toreno's credit rating with the law-boys in New York. Finally she gave it back to me, puffed vigorously at her cigarette and said,

'You have to admit, Mr. Preston, when I decide to get taken in, I do one hell of a good job.'

'No use blaming yourself too much. It's a far cry from Palmside Boulevard to the East River. Toreno doesn't advertise his record, after all.'

'I know you're only being nice, but thank you.' She held up the clipping.

'This is interesting too, isn't it? The part about him having been married once? Wonder who she was.'

'Or is,' I corrected. 'If there'd been any proceedings to obtain a divorce, Joe Armstrong would have dug it out.'

'H'm,' she mused. 'I'd give a lot to have half-an-hour's conversation with the mysterious Elizabeth. She must have been quite a girl.'

It was ten a.m. and I knew it wouldn't be long before the Monkton City cops would be breathing down my neck, asking how much longer I was going to keep them waiting at headquarters. The sudden clanging of the phone interrupted my thoughts. I picked it up.

'Miss Digby, if it's the police tell them I haven't arrived yet.'

'It's not the police,' she replied distantly. 'It's a man who won't tell me his name.'

Anonymous telephone calls usually mean information. Right now I could use some.

'Put him on.'

There was some clicking, finally a man said,

'Am I speaking to Mr. Mark Preston?' The voice was clipped and precise.

'In person,' I answered. 'Who're you?'

'Hold the line one moment, please.'

I looked across at Moira and shrugged to indicate I didn't know who was at the other end of the phone. She sat there trying to look like somebody who was not over-hearing a private conversation.

'Mr. Preston?'

This was a new voice, deep and authoritative.

'Speaking,' I confirmed.

'We haven't met, but I believe you'll have heard of me,' he announced. 'My name is Marsland Freeman.'

'The Second?'

I hadn't intended to be rude. It just came out automatically. He chose to ignore it.

'I'm calling from my house at Rock Beach. You know the area?'

'Yes, Mr. Freeman, I know it well. From the outside that is.'

'This is your opportunity to correct that, Mr. Preston. There is a matter I should like to discuss with you. Could you manage to be here, say, at ten-thirty this morning?'

This was one for the book. An appointment with Marsland Freeman II, and he has to pick a time when I'm due at police headquarters to discuss other matters. Matters of murder.

'I'm sorry, Mr. Freeman, but I'm expected at police headquarters this morning. I can't afford to skip it. Could you suggest any other time?'

'There will be no difficulty with the

police authorities, Mr. Preston. One of my attorneys will explain to them.'

No difficulty at police headquarters. Just like that. It must be nice to have forty-seven million dollars.

'Well, O.K., if you're sure there'll be no trouble. They don't want me for a parking offence. There are two murders under investigation.'

'Really.' He didn't sound very impressed. 'Then I'll expect you in thirty minutes.'

'I'll be there,' I said, and hated myself. What I should have said was something about freedom and the rights of the individual or some such. Nobody has any right to order anybody else about that way. If I'd been half a man I'd have said I was too busy. But I didn't. I said I'd be there.

Moira Chase had abandoned any pretence of not listening to the conversation.

'*The* Freeman?' she queried. 'Lois's father?'

'The same.' I nodded. 'Wants to see me in half an hour.'

'I see. But the police, they won't like you keeping them waiting, will they?'

'No, ma'am, they won't. They won't like it at all, but they'll swallow it. Because Mr. Freeman says they'll swallow it. Because Mr. Freeman owns one half of the planet Earth, and if anybody tries to be difficult with him they are liable to have a very hard time. Including the Monkton City police force.'

'And a certain private investigator?'

I bowed slightly.

'Me too. If I don't please all the people all the time I go out of business very fast indeed. Something to do with a licence I have to have before I'm allowed to operate.'

'I'm sorry, I didn't mean to be sarcastic.'

'I know it.' I made a great display of looking at my watch. 'Mrs. Chase, I'm going to ask you to do something you'll find hard.'

'What is it? Anything at all that will help to find Ellen.'

'It's nothing. Nothing at all. I want you to go on home and rest. There isn't anything more useful you can be doing right this minute than sitting in a comfortable chair near the telephone.'

'But there must be something useful — '

'That will be useful. If Mr. Lytton or
any of Fordham's men want you in a
hurry, how can they get hold of you if
you're chasing all over the state?'

'I can't argue with that, of course. Do
you really think they may have found out
where she is by this time?'

I heaved my shoulders.

'Quien sabe? I'd like to say yes, but I
just don't know. I'll tell you this much.
After I've seen Freeman I'm going to a
place where they may know something
about Ellen.'

'Where?' she pleaded. 'Please tell me.
Perhaps if I went there right away — '

'They'd tell you nothing. I'm sorry. I
told you yours was the hard part. I'll try
to call you around noon. Don't wait after
one o'clock. If I haven't called by then
you'll know I'm in a jam of some kind.'

'What shall I do if I don't hear?'

'Call the police. Talk to Lieutenant
John Rourke. Nobody else. Tell him
everything that's happened. Don't leave

out a thing. And tell Mr. Lytton you're bringing in the law.'

She nodded.

'All right.' She stood up. 'I'll be right beside the phone. Good luck.'

I was afraid she might bust out crying again.

'Thanks. Try not to worry. I'm sure this'll work out.'

It sounded so full of confidence I almost believed it myself.

8

When Marsland Freeman II talked about
his house being at Rock Beach he was
trying to be unostentatious. His house
was Rock Beach, or rather the house and
surrounding area were. He owned the
whole headland, a long low promontory
that stuck arrogantly out into the Pacific
Ocean, as if to proclaim that any ocean
wishing to wash away any property
belonging to Mr. Freeman had just better
try. After twenty minutes' driving I turned
off the main coastal highway into the
private road leading to the house. Half a
mile further on I left the wooded area
behind and emerged into a flat expanse of
rocky country with bushes cunningly
planted in sheltered spots to take the
bareness out of what nature had produced.

I could see the house in the distance, a
rugged-looking building of grey stone.
There was an area of green around the

outside, and I remembered the local stories of how soil had been carried for miles to create an artificial garden on top of the cliffs. I came to a slight turn in the road. When I rounded it there was a figure of a woman just up ahead standing in the path of the car. I eased on the brake and pulled up just short of her. It was Lois Freeman. Today she wore a red-check lumber-jack shirt and some green denim tight pants. Her hair was combed loosely back from her ears and the green eyes regarded me with amusement.

'Morning,' she greeted. 'How about a lift up to the house?'

I pushed the door open.

'It's your house, lady. If I refused you'd probably have me ejected by the third under-butler.'

She slid gracefully in beside me. I caught a faint whiff of perfume from her.

'Don't you know beautiful girls ought not to thumb rides on the highway. An awful lot of trouble starts that way.'

'I don't see how I can get into any trouble with you,' she pouted. 'Last night

I tried to pick you up in a bar, and all I got that time was the cold shoulder.'

'Miss Freeman,' I began.

'Lois,' she corrected. 'You're Mark, aren't you?'

'Lois,' I said, 'I'm here to see your father. On business, so he says.'

'I know. I told him about you.'

'Told him what about me?'

'Oh, things. Anyway he went to the trouble of phoning you, didn't he?'

'He did. I'm having a great time lately. Last night a famous heiress practically solicited me in a bar, today a millionaire calls me up personally to go see him. To top it off, famous heiress meets me to kind of cheer me in. What's the pitch?'

She bit her lip.

'Are you always hard to get on with, like this?'

I sighed.

'Lady, I am the easiest guy in the world to get along with. Ask anybody. They'll all tell you about old Mark Preston, the people's friend. But that's with people. The kind of money you and your father have knocks you out of my usual circle of acquaintances. Why should either of you be interested in me? I'm nothing special.'

'Maybe not. I really don't know you well enough to pass an opinion on that, do I?'

Her attitude was cooler. I wondered whether I wasn't being a little touchy today. She was very close to me in the seat, and I knew that if it weren't for all that money I would be taking a very different line.

'All right, I guess I asked for that,' I admitted. 'It was nice of you to meet me.'

'Fine,' she was cheerful again. 'Anyhow, I made some progress this time.'

'You did?'

'Of course. The moment I got in you said I was beautiful.'

So I had to grin. I turned my head to get a look at her face. She was smiling too. Then we were at the front of the house and the brief moment of intimacy was gone. Lois climbed out and I followed.

'Dad'll be in the library,' she told me. 'He always sees everybody in there. It's the only time he ever goes near the place.

His reading is confined strictly to stock market reports.'

I followed her up the wide shallow steps and in through the heavy brass-bound oak door. It was cool in the vast hall. For the first time it struck me that the only living soul I'd seen all the way to the house had been Lois.

'I thought very rich people always had armed guards and dogs and stuff to keep out undesirable callers,' I said to Lois. I realised that I was almost whispering.

'Everybody knew you were expected,' she returned. 'People here don't wave their presence about unless it's required. Try to get in some time when nobody knows you're coming.'

'Oh,' I said.

We'd been walking along the hallway. Lois stopped now beside a closed door. The handle was a heavy ring of worked iron, similar to the doors on the old missions.

'This is it,' she announced. 'All set?'

I nodded, and followed her inside.

'This is Mark Preston, father. I'll be around if you want me.'

She slipped out past me and I heard the door close. The library was lined on three walls with books that reached right up to the ceiling. The fourth wall was largely taken up by an old-style stone fireplace flanked on either side by windows. At one of these a man sat in a solid leather chair. Now he rose and came towards me.

'You're punctual, Mr. Preston. It's a good beginning.'

He didn't offer to shake hands. Marsland Freeman was a man of sixty plus, tall and upright. His build was rugged and the shock of white hair was beginning to thin a little. The bushy eyebrows were almost military in their bristling fierceness. He was as I'd imagined him to be, big, tough, aggressive. The voice, commanding enough on the telephone, now made me feel I ought to be standing at attention while he listed my recent misdeeds. A ridiculous feeling. I tried to shrug it off, after all, he was only a man when you came right down to it.

'You sent for me, Mr. Freeman.' I made

it a flat statement.

'I did. Will you have a drink?'

'Thanks. I can always use a scotch.'

He opened a glass-fronted cupboard. Inside were a selection of bottles and decanters. Turning slightly over one shoulder he said,

'Say when.'

I said when. He helped himself to a weak mixture of the same and sipped at it.

'Hah,' he cleared his throat. 'Good. Well now, let's sit down.'

He took one of the deep armchairs that stood before the empty fireplace. I perched in the other one and found it comfortable.

'Do you mind if I smoke?' I asked.

'Please do. I don't myself these days. Medical advice, you know, but I like to see others enjoy it. There's an ashtray by your elbow.'

I parked the glass on the arm of the chair while I took out my Old Favourites and lit one.

'I approve of your brand, Mr. Preston. Every tenth packet you buy earns me one cent. It doesn't sound a lot, but believe me it adds up.'

'Yes, I can imagine it would.'

Now I had everything. Drink, chair, smoke, ashtray. Now we had to come to it.

'Now, Mr. Preston, let us get down to business.' He fixed the piercing blue eyes on me. 'According to my daughter Lois, you are a very unusual man.'

'Why do you say that?' I asked.

'Because according to her, you refused a thousand dollars last night in exchange for some trivial piece of information she wanted.'

'What's so unusual about that?' I countered.

'It is unusual to find someone who will retain an ethic at the sacrifice of a thousand dollars. Believe me, if it were common practice I should not be entertaining you in these surroundings this morning. However, as you say, it is not exactly unique. But Lois also tells me she used her charms on you into the bargain. Those charms are not inconsiderable, and yet you remained firm. When she told me this I became interested in you.'

'Really? From what point of view?' I took another sip of the scotch. It was the kind they all pretend they are in the ads.

'I'm a business man. My interests are wide. I have become what I am largely as a result of judging people. I have had a number of lifelong rules. One of them is this; when I see a man I can trust with money and women, I hire him. No matter what it costs, I have to have that man. It is a rule which has repaid me handsomely over the years.'

It wasn't easy to decide whether he was trying to impress me, or whether he automatically thought of himself as a kind of god-symbol.

'Sounds like a sensible rule,' I replied. 'How does it apply in my case?'

'I've had enquiries made about you through one or two local sources. Very good reports, very good indeed.'

'Tell me,' I said curiously. 'What have the local sources got to say?'

'They say you're an honest man. A bit tough, but I don't mind that. Cynical too, but that's an asset in my organisation. And so I'm going to make you an offer, Mr. Preston.'

'I'm always open to offers, Mr. Freeman,' I told him.

'Good. One of my companies is a beef-canning plant in Brazil. I'm having a lot of trouble down there, labour disturbances chiefly, but also some sabotage from time to time. My local manager has fallen down on the job. He's out. I need somebody to get down there immediately, straighten things out.'

He broke off, and waited for a contribution from me.

'The beef-canning industry is a little off my usual beat,' I told him. 'Wouldn't you normally need someone who knows a bit about the job?'

The white head jerked up and down in agreement.

'Naturally. You would be quite unfitted for the manager's position. I don't want you to interfere with the running of the business. The staff can carry on until I get a replacement down. What you will do is to find out which other people are interfering with it. Find them, stop them. Are you interested?'

'Isn't it customary to mention money on occasions like this?'

His smile was brief.

'You would receive manager's pay while you were there. During your absence my personnel people will investigate you thoroughly to see whether we can offer you anything permanent when you return. If that should not be possible, we could make it one lump payment for the whole period.'

'Amounting to how much exactly?'

'Twenty thousand dollars.'

I sat very quietly thinking about twenty thousand dollars. The deal was an obvious frame-up. To do him justice, I don't believe Freeman expected me to fall for it. The story I mean, not the twenty grand. He thought that would hit the spot, and I'd forgive the fairy tales. While I was trying to imagine what all that money would look like spread out on the floor, a shadow crossed the window. I looked up quickly, to see a wheelchair passing by outside. The woman seated in it was turned away from me looking out to sea. There was a beefy-looking man in a white linen uniform pushing the chair along. I didn't pay much attention. I was still busy thinking.

'You haven't answered me,' said the millionaire. 'I shouldn't have thought there was very much need to think too deeply over such an offer. You don't get one like it every day.'

'No. You misunderstand me, Mr. Freeman. I'm not sitting here wondering whether to accept or not. I'm trying to guess why you made it.'

He fidgeted in his chair. With discomfort, not embarrassment.

'Been through all that already. Now then, what makes you hesitate?'

'Hesitate?'

I rose slowly, controlling the irritation which I knew must be showing in my tone.

'If your performance this morning is any pointer to how you came by all those millions, Mr. Freeman, you can keep 'em. Just who do you think you are?'

His voice was even. Never do business

in a bad mood, as they say.

'I am a man who just made you a very reasonable offer. Do you always get excited like this?'

I took a deep breath. Already I was way past my ears. Preston the P.I. was all washed up. This man would have my licence to light a cigar with. So I might as well do it up brown.

'You're crude, Freeman, plain crude. Here's twenty thousand dollars. Get lost in Brazil for a couple of months. There are one or two matters here in Monkton City which I will attend to while you're away.'

I made a poor attempt to mimic his voice. His eyes turned to stone but he made no answer. I pointed at him accusingly.

'Your daughter made an honest effort to find out what I was up to last night. She laid a thousand bucks on the line, no hypocrisy, and told me she wanted in. It didn't work, so you said never mind. We'll get the poor slob up here this morning. I'll tell him what an honest face he has, they always love that bit, then I'll bribe him to go away. Well I'm telling you what to do with your money. Another thing, some police wanted to see me today. They're only working on murder cases, and you'll have their badges if they question where I've been but you know something? They're honest men too. Just hard-working, everyday coppers, but they're honest. You needn't think you would have solved anything even if you had got rid of me. Rourke, and the rest down at headquarters, they'll come up with the answers just the same. You want some advice, here it is. Spend your money on legal talent. That's where it'll do most good when I get through telling what I know.'

'And exactly what do you know?' he asked softly.

'Plenty. I know that in 1957 the New York Police thought they solved three murders when they gunned Giovanni Toreno off the Brooklyn Bridge. I know they were wrong that time. I know about Elizabeth being married to his brother Vic — '

A look of pain crossed his face at the

last part. He passed a weary hand across his forehead. I rushed ahead.

'I know the killings have started again. When I tell them my story, the police will soon tie the whole thing up.'

Marsland Freeman looked up quickly.

'Started again? What do you mean by that?'

He was so eager, he forgot to pretend he didn't know what I was talking about.

'I'm talking about a fat slob named Wiener, known as Little-boy, and the girl Fay who was cut up last night — '

'Last night? You're sure, absolutely sure?'

He was on his feet, hand tugging at my sleeve.

'Mr. Freeman,' I stared him levelly in the eye, 'I saw the girl. Afterwards. Saw what was done to her.'

Then he did something completely unexpected. Letting go of my arm, he sat down heavily in the chair, burying his face in his hands. His body was shaking. I should have felt some kind of triumph. All of a sudden I seemed to be holding the cards. It was me standing upright, while the multi-millionaire sat with his head bowed. Instead I felt a helpless bewilderment at the sudden turn of events, and something else besides, a feeling of pity for him. Without knowing any reason for it, I felt pity. He soon pulled himself together.

'Forgive me, Mr. Preston.' His voice was almost back to normal. 'I have had a number of shocks today. I don't seem capable of withstanding such things the way I could twenty years ago. Please, won't you sit down again? I can understand your annoyance, but perhaps when I've told you the whole story, you'll feel differently.'

He wasn't telling now. He was asking. I resumed my seat facing him, and waited. He coughed slightly.

'I have two daughters, Mr. Preston. When their mother died I had to make up my mind whether it would be better for them if I married again or not. I decided against it. My elder daughter Elizabeth — '

Elizabeth. He stressed the name and looked to see if I reacted. I didn't ' — was just thirteen. Lois was almost ten. The loss of their mother was a great blow to them both, naturally. Elizabeth was always a headstrong, self-willed child. She was inconsolable. I did as much as I could to fill the gap, but at the same time I could not neglect my business interests. Elizabeth began to get into trouble at school. I was asked to take her away from three of them. There was even one particularly wild outbreak where I had to exert considerable influence to stop the police from bringing charges. When she finally finished with school she led a reckless life. I tried every way possible to bring her to her senses, but she had begun some time earlier to resent me. She felt in some way that I was responsible for her mother's death. So the parties got wilder and the drinking was out of all control. She had to have medical treatment for alcoholism when she was twenty years old.'

He was talking half to me, half to himself. There was no bitterness in his voice, no resentment. Just sadness. For him Elizabeth would always be a thirteen-year-old kid who lost her mother.

'When she came of age she also became financially independent. I'd arranged a number of trusts for both girls, years before. Well, Elizabeth left home. She went to New York, and none of us heard any more of her for eighteen months. She didn't use the family name there, so there was nobody to connect her with us. Not among the kind of people with whom she chose to mix.'

He broke off.

'Please help yourself to another drink, if you wish.'

'No thanks, one was plenty. Did you manage to fill in the details of what happened during the time she was in New York?'

He nodded slowly.

'Oh, yes. It took time but gradually we built up a picture. A picture of rottenness and depravity, things far in excess of anything that ever happened while she was home. She had become,' he faltered, 'become a drug addict. Not even in a mild form. Elizabeth was never one for half-measures. She was injecting pure heroin into her veins.'

Main lining. No half-measures indeed.

'The effects of this vary, apparently, from one person to another. Some go to sleep, some get maudlin, a few go mildly sex-mad. Elizabeth became violent. On one occasion she half-wrecked a bar. She was sentenced to two months' imprisonment that time.'

I was beginning to understand why I'd felt pity for the old man a few minutes earlier.

'Among the riff-raff she associated with was a man named Toreno, Vic Toreno. He was a criminal with a long police record. This man knew that Elizabeth had a considerable private fortune. It suited him to catch my daughter on one of her wild sprees and they were married. What sort of marriage it was God knows. They must have made a pretty pair. Oh, please don't look surprised. I love my daughter, but by that time I had no illusions left about what she'd become. I knew her, or thought I did. I had not at that time heard the worst.'

He picked up his glass. It was empty. I

rose and took it from him, went to the cupboard and poured him another drink.

'Thank you.'

He took a sip at it, sat cradling the glass between his hands.

He was obviously coming to the part that was really tough to tell.

'Then, in March, 1957, the crowning blow came. My daughter killed a woman.'

Without looking at me, he hurried out the last few words and put the glass to his lips. When he set it down it was empty.

'Do you mean it was murder?' I tried to sound surprised.

'Yes. The woman was some showgirl named Eleanor Candy. I don't know why Elizabeth killed her, but it was some mad quarrel I assume. Elizabeth doesn't know either. She admits she was full of these vile drugs at the time. All she remembers is standing over the dead girl with this knife in her hand. Her husband's,' his tone was edged, 'brother was in the room. He took the knife away from her, got her out of the place.'

'I see. A public place?'

'No. The girl's apartment. This brother

took Elizabeth to her husband and told him what had happened. The husband questioned her about it, then said he would have to contact me. He had found out who his wife's father was long before, of course. It's one thing to preserve an anonymous identity when living alone. Quite another matter to attempt it with a marriage partner. Even such a marriage partner.'

'So Toreno contacted you?' I put in.

'Yes. He telephoned me at once. Said I had to go to New York if I wanted to see my daughter alive again. I needed no second asking. He gave me to understand that he meant it. I flew up at once. He took me to Elizabeth. I was shocked when I saw her. I believe that but for this dreadful business of the girl's murder, Elizabeth would probably not have had long to live anyway. Not without medical care.'

He got up from the chair. He was agitated again, reliving the New York visit of years before.

'Elizabeth told me what she'd done. I suppose my duty was to call the police and hand my daughter over to them. Wouldn't you say, Preston?'

He cocked his head to one side and waited for my reply.

'Duty,' I said carefully, 'is a term bandied about by people who sit outside the area of decision. I haven't a daughter, but if I had I wouldn't want to have to make such a decision.'

It seemed to satisfy Freeman.

'Exactly. Now I'll tell you what I did. I told Toreno that I was prepared to listen to any scheme he might have that would save my daughter's life. Anything at all. Toreno had already got his proposition ready. It was this. There was a sex-killer loose in New York. Some maniac who'd already killed two women. That was fact one. Fact two was that his brother, Giovanni, the one who'd taken Elizabeth away from the girl's apartment, had been careless with some recent criminal activities. He didn't say what they were, but it wouldn't be long before the police would catch up with him. When they did he would face a stiff sentence, a minimum of ten years in the State penitentiary. Toreno then told me his proposition. His brother would mutilate the corpse so that it appeared to be another sex murder. Then word would be got to the police that Giovanni Toreno was the man they wanted. He would run away when questioned and appear to be killed in a fight. The police would consider the case closed and Elizabeth would go free.'

'And the brothers Toreno would head for California,' I muttered.

'Yes. Not as brothers of course. The young one had to have an extensive operation carried out on his face so that no one would be likely to recognise him. Then he dyed his hair and simply changed his name.'

'To Kenny Napoli,' I finished.

Freeman was startled.

'How did you know that?'

'I didn't really. Just guessing good this morning. Tell me the rest of it, Mr. Freeman.'

'That's almost the end of it. I brought Elizabeth home. She has had the finest medical attention ever since. The doctors can't promise that she'll ever enjoy good health again, but they think she might leave the wheel-chair behind in perhaps another six months.'

So the woman in the chair had been Elizabeth Freeman. I felt a tremendous curiosity to see her face.

'Toreno, of course, has never left me alone. He demands money, legal protection, continually. I pay gladly. Then a few months ago he got this idea of running a casino here in Monkton City. It wasn't hard for him to persuade me to help him.'

'Tell me, did he give any reason for that? I mean, according to my information he was riding the big wheel up in San Francisco.'

The white head moved from side to side.

'No. No reason.'

'I see. Well, Mr. Freeman, you've been very frank with me. I don't want to seem ungracious, but could I ask why?'

He reached inside his jacket and pulled out a thick brown envelope.

'Because of this,' he tapped at it with his forefinger. 'This, and the fact that you know so much already. When the police hear how much you've found out, I'm quite certain you are correct in assuming they will soon piece the rest of the story together.'

That was true enough.

'What's so special about the envelope?' I queried.

'It contains documents. This man you killed yesterday, Wiener — '

'Hold on,' I interrupted. 'I didn't kill Wiener.'

'That does not agree with my information. However, it is irrelevant — '

'Like hell it is,' I snapped. 'There's nothing irrelevant to me about the gas-chamber. I'm not going to sit in it for something I didn't do.'

'Please, Mr. Preston, don't keep interrupting. Let us assume then, that you did not kill the man. He was killed, that is the important factor.'

I scowled a little but didn't say anything.

'Wiener was an associate of Toreno's from the New York days. It was, in fact, he who identified the substitute body of Giovanni Toreno. Mr. Wiener had taken certain precautions against the possibility of an early death. As an accomplice in the faked death of Giovanni he regarded himself as a danger to the Torenos. Not an enviable position to be in. So Wiener left with a prominent firm of New York attorneys a statement explaining the whole affair. This was in a sealed package of course, to be opened in the event of his meeting a violent death. The attorneys were to take photostat copies and then hand the original to the New York police.'

'So Toreno didn't dare to bump him off, because he knew it would be the end for Giovanni,' I was talking half to myself.

'And not only Giovanni. Toreno had made himself an accessory after the fact of murder, don't forget. If he didn't actually receive a death sentence he would spend many years in prison,' pointed out Freeman.

'Are you telling me these attorneys double-crossed Wiener and sent the statement to you?' I enquired.

'No, not exactly,' he returned. 'But they saw my daughter's name in the statement. They are anxious that I should not misunderstand their actions. So they sent me one of the copies, together with an assurance that my daughter's name will receive every consideration on the part of those concerned.'

I couldn't work out what that might mean, so I took the envelope from his extended hand, smoothed out the contents and began to read.

Little-boy Wiener might not have been a literary genius, but with the stuff he put down on paper he didn't need to be. The statement consisted of dynamite in word form. In the year 1957 Wiener had been strictly small beer around New York, but he had ambitions. The Toreno brothers on the other hand were up-and-coming. Vic Toreno's wife, Elizabeth, was a heavy drug-taker. Sometimes she would pass out for as long as two whole days. On these occasions Toreno parked her at the apartment of a showgirl named Cuddles Candy. Cuddles was by way of being an occasional friend of Giovanni Toreno. Wiener was her more steady boy-friend. It gave Wiener some kind of a kick to know that his woman spent part of her time with a rising character like Giovanni. The only complication was that he had to be careful when he put in an appearance at Cuddles' apartment in case the younger Toreno was there. On the night of March 17 Wiener went to see the lady. Toreno's car was in the garage, so he waited outside. There was a scream, and soon after that Giovanni and Elizabeth Toreno left the building. Elizabeth seemed to be doped up to the eyebrows. After they left Wiener went up to the apartment. Cuddles was dead when he got there, butchered in the same way as other recent Broadway girl victims. Wiener put two and two together, wrote out his statement for posterity, and went to see Vic Toreno. The first statement finished at that point. There was another, dateline one month later confessing to his part in the false identification of a corpse as being that of Giovanni Toreno. Also a mild case of theft of a corpse from the morgue, the one which was dumped in the river, complete with bullet wounds, to do Giovanni's hitch in the next world. It was Wiener's second trip to the river, since he had also assisted in dumping the deceased Cuddles in the same stretch of water.

Marsland Freeman interrupted.

'What do you make of it?'

'It reads well. I couldn't put it down,' I told him. 'You won't have missed the significance of this story?'

'I don't know. At first I thought it would clear Elizabeth. Something I can assure you I never dreamed possible. But I've talked to one of my attorneys, in the third person of course. He tells me that there is nothing in a statement like that which will bear any examination in a court of law. It does not exonerate Elizabeth at all, merely fixes her at the scene of a crime.'

I was impatient to get in my two cents-worth.

'But, Mr. Freeman, Wiener swears the girl was mutilated at the time of death. According to you Toreno — Vic I mean — offered to arrange for this to be done hours afterwards. He had to sell you that proposition because he knew the girl had already died that way. Because he knew Giovanni really was the sex-maniac. I expect Giovanni just pulled Elizabeth up from her sleep, stood her over the body and stuck a knife in her hand. Believe me, I've had some experience with these people. When they're really gone it would be easy to fool one with a stunt like that.'

He nodded vigorously.

'Agreed. I am now convinced that is a true picture of what really happened, but there is still insufficient evidence in law. My first real hope is the news you brought just now, about some other poor girl having been murdered last night. If we can find Giovanni and prove he committed that crime — '

His voice trailed away.

'I think I might be able to find him,' I said.

Freeman looked like a man in a dream. He spoke slowly.

'I'm not going to try to impress you with my money. It doesn't seem to have much effect. Go and get Giovanni for me, Mr. Preston. Please.'

I went across to the window. The wheelchair was parked in a small area of grass. The seated woman stared out across the ocean. She looked old, tired and old. Freeman was standing next to me.

'That is my daughter Elizabeth. She is twenty-six years old.'

He said it simply, and it had more impact that way. Whatever Elizabeth had done a few years earlier, she had paid for it. Was paying now. I turned away.

'I'm going to try for Giovanni, Mr. Freeman, but not for you. For a girl named Fay.'

'Fay? I don't think I follow. Fay whom?'

'That's the funny part, I don't even know her last name. She's the one Giovanni killed last night. She was nobody, a good-hearted tramp with a voice like a cement-mixer. But she deserved a better break than that. I only ever talked to her once but I saw her after he got through. You think I'm crazy?'

He didn't answer that. Maybe he did think I was crazy. Maybe I was, at that. When I reached the door he called,

'Mr. Preston. Good luck.'

I found my way as far as the front door. Lois Freeman was sitting outside on the steps.

'Leaving now?' she enquired.

'Yes.'

I went and climbed into the car. She followed and got in beside me.

'I can't take you into town,' I said. 'I'm not headed that way.'

'Don't be so ungracious. I'll get off at the highway and walk back.'

I sighed and gunned the motor.

'Mind if I ask you a question?' she demanded.

'Uh, uh,' I negatived.

'What's wrong with me?'

'How do you mean, wrong with you?'

'You know damned well what I mean. I'm the right height and weight. I stick out where it's expected, and to the required extent. Some men have even thought I was quite nice to look at.' She sounded indignant.

'All right, so you're quite nice to look at. It's all I can do to stop myself grabbing you right now and dragging you to the nearest bed. Is that better?'

I squinted sideways to get a look at her reaction. She bit her lip.

'A little. But Mark,' she put a hand on

my arm, 'you are still managing to stop yourself.'

I stopped the car, turned and pulled her towards me. I didn't have to pull too hard. Her nails were pain at the back of my neck.

'Is that better?' I repeated.

'Much better,' she was talking into the front of my jacket.

'All right, you won your point. Now out,' I ordered.

'Out?'

'Out.'

With a puzzled frown she got out of the car and shut the door.

'I don't understand you,' she remarked.

'Yes you do. You understand me just fine. What you mean is you don't want to. You don't want to know that there's anybody in the whole wide world who could resist all that money combined with a package like you. Well there is. Me. I want you all right, but I don't make a sucker out of myself for you or anybody else. I'll stay my side of the fence. It's poorer over there, but I don't owe anybody.'

I went to push the starter.

'No, wait, please. Don't I get a chance to put my point of view?'

'Sorry, I can't stop,' I said brusquely.

'You're wrong, Mark. You're making a mistake.'

I stared woodenly out at the road. She made a gesture of impatience.

'Oh, you're impossible. What's so important you have to rush off like this? Where are you going anyway?'

I eased off the brake and started to roll.

'I'm going to kill a man,' I told her.

Schoolkid. I could have bitten it back almost before the words were out. Lois stood in the centre of the road watching me. I could see her in the rear mirror. If anybody had asked what made me act that way with her I wouldn't have known the answer. Somewhere we got off on the wrong foot and I'd been dancing badly ever since. Not even I thought it was her fault. And that last part. That was from hunger. 'I'm going to kill a man', he said evenly, between his strong white teeth. That was from the one about the guy who finally discovered the identity of the

261

officer who had planted the missing cigarette case in his quarters and caused him to be cashiered from the regiment, etc. Kill a man. Ha ha. What was likely going to happen to me was that a couple of Toreno's gorillas would rough me up and I'd spend a few days with my face in plaster.

At that more realistic thought I rested my left arm lightly on the wheel. It was reassuring to feel the derringer digging into the flesh. I headed for Palmside Boulevard, known as Millions Mile.

9

There was some traffic on the road and it was past noon when I hit the private roadway to the Alhambra. I took it easy knowing that the gates were not far along. They were still there, but standing wide open and secured to wooden posts either side. Evidently the precautions were not considered necessary this early in the day. I drove up to the parking lot and got out. There were seven other cars already there, the only one I recognised being the white sedan Vic Toreno had been driving the day before. The front of the house was deserted but somebody must have spotted me from a window. As I walked in at the open front door I suddenly found my way blocked by the massive A1. Today he didn't smile.

'You're pushing it too hard, Preston. Last night I would have said you were lucky. Your luck just ran out.'

'Never mind the chatter, A1. Just take me to Toreno.'

'Don't worry. That's where you're going.'

The short-snouted automatic was held loosely against my stomach while be patted around my coat. Not so loosely that I got any heroic ideas. The thought of an ounce of steel-jacketed lead ploughing its way through my entrails was enough to discourage any foolish thoughts. A1 found the .38, grunted as he plucked it out, then jerked his head towards the stairs.

'Up,' he ordered. 'I'll be behind you.'

I went up, and at the top headed for the room where I'd had my talk with Toreno the night before. At the door A1 pushed me aside and stuck his head into the room.

'You got a visitor, boss. Preston's out here.'

There was a mumble of talk from within the room. A1 pulled out his head.

'All right, Jack. Inside.'

In case I couldn't find the entrance he gave me a shove in the back. I almost lost my footing and was well into the centre of the room before I pulled up.

Toreno sat behind the desk as before. Today he wore a coloured silk shirt open at the neck. Close at hand, in a chair against the wall, sat Kent Shubert. Standing by the window was Ellen Chase, dressed as I'd seen her the previous morning. She looked slightly flushed, as though with excitement. The two men stared at me without expression.

'Well, well,' I said softly, 'the brothers Toreno.'

Kent Shubert, or I should say Giovanni Toreno, clicked his teeth impatiently.

'You see what I mean, Vic? This guy has gotta go.'

Vic made no reply but went on looking me over with that stony expression. I said,

'Don't be childish, Giovanni. You're in plenty enough trouble already.'

Then Vic spoke. His voice was quiet. It gave me the shivers.

'Tell us about that, Preston. Tell us what kind of trouble we're in already.'

'Take your choice,' I replied. 'Murder of one kind and another. You can elect New York and try the chair, or you can stay right here in sunny California and give the gas-chamber some business.'

Vic smiled. He had a fine set of teeth. All the better to eat me with, I reflected.

'Crazy talk. And that's all it is, just talk. Murder? You're nuts. What else you got besides talk?'

'I just left your father-in-law. He told me a long story.'

'Oh, you know about my father-in-law?' replied Vic. 'Well, you don't want to take any notice of his stories. He imagines all kinds of things. If he didn't have all that dough they'd have locked him up years ago.'

I nodded, as if agreeing.

'You're quite right. This story he told me was strong on imagination. Only it wasn't his imagination. It was yours.'

The smile disappeared.

'Don't talk smart. Just say what you mean.'

Giovanni started to chip in.

'Vic, why don't I just — '

'Shut up, Joe,' commanded Toreno. 'Let's have it, peeper.'

'I was telling you about this yarn I got

from Mr. Freeman. You told him a wicked story, Vittorio.'

I wagged a reproving finger.

'You told him Elizabeth killed Eleanor Candy.'

'That's right, I did. You don't believe me, ask the cripple. She'll tell you the same thing herself.'

'Yes,' I agreed. 'I know she will. Because she was full of heroin at the time. You could have told that girl she burnt down the White House and she'd buy it. It was bad luck for you about Little-boy.'

'What about him?'

Vic was still composed.

'This is all news to you of course. Little-boy was outside Cuddles' apartment waiting for this specimen to leave,' I indicated Giovanni. 'He went up there as soon as Elizabeth and your precious brother left. Cuddles was dead all right, cut to glory into the bargain. Only it wasn't your wife killed her, it was Giovanni here.'

Giovanni was beginning to get agitated. His fingers kept pulling at the cloth of his pants and his eyes were moving from side to side rapidly.

'I tell you, Vic — ' he began.

'In a minute, Joe. What kinda yarn is that.' Vic turned back to me. 'Wiener tell you that?'

'No. He told the District Attorney in New York. I've seen a copy of his statement. A sworn statement from a dead man. That's strong meat in our courtrooms.'

'Nah.' He waved a derisive hand. 'Nothing to it. All those years back. Nobody'd buy that.'

'They'd buy the part of the statement that says Giovanni is still alive,' I pointed out.

'Why would they? It ain't true. This here is a piano-player named Kent Shubert. I don't know nothing about the guy, 'cept he plays piano in one of my joints. Yesterday he walked out on me. How do I know where he went? Where do piano-players go? A picture of him? What would I be doing with a picture of a piano-player?'

He smiled again. Running over the

story out loud had given him further confidence in it. It sounded all right. He jabbed a stubby forefinger in my direction.

'And don't think they're going to get too tough with Freeman. Any kind of investigation into what happened back there in New York wouldn't be healthy for my dear wife. They won't strike much oil in that direction.'

He leaned back, very satisfied with himself. In his chair by the wall Giovanni was beginning to mutter to himself. Vic looked at him darkly but it didn't have any visible effect. At the window Ellen didn't seem to be paying any attention to what went on in the room. Her eyes were large and bright, and the flush on her face stayed the same colour. So far, she'd given no indication that she'd noticed me.

'As for me, they haven't got a thing on me. Not a thing. The only guy around here who's in trouble is you, peeper. The law ain't so dumb they'll leave you walking around much longer. You shoulda played it smart yesterday. Once your buddy turned you loose over the Little-boy thing, you shoulda made tracks.

Rourke won't be able to keep 'em off your back much longer.'

I grinned at him. He didn't like it.

'You know, Vic, where your little brother is concerned you have a blind spot. You only see what you want to see. I didn't kill Little-boy. Told you that last night.'

'Haw, haw. Very funny. You're standing there with the cannon still in your fist when this copper walks in, but you didn't kill Little-boy. All right,' he was expansive. 'Who did? Don't tell me Elizabeth finally made it out of that chair?'

We were getting down to the real Vic Toreno now. All his pretensions, his acquired good-joe airs were gone. We were back with the man who clawed and kicked his way out of the jungle on the East Side of New York. Even his language was different.

'All right, smart boy,' I said softly. 'I'll tell you who gunned Wiener. Little brother here. He did it.'

Vic laughed shortly.

'Crazy. Hey, Joe, tell this guy he's crazy.'

270

Giovanni half-raised his head. The thick black hair was soaked with perspiration and hung damply forward over his forehead. Beads of sweat stood out all over his face. His features were contorting into odd lines. From his lips came sounds, strange, half-strangled animal noises. At once Vic got up and went across to him, kneeling beside him and cradling his shoulders with his arms.

'It's all right, Joe Joe. Vic is right here, boy. It's all right.'

His voice was gentle, soothing. Gone were the harsh inflections and the edged tones. He looked across at me with fury in his eyes, patting at his brother's head with his free hand.

'You've done this,' he hissed. 'I'll get around to you when he's better.'

At the change of tone Giovanni began to cry, sobs that shook his body violently, while the great tears rolled down his face and splashed unheeded against Vic's protecting chest. The elder Toreno whispered soothingly into his ear, rocking him slightly back and forth. I felt revulsion.

Ellen Chase looked around suddenly

from the window and saw the brothers. She didn't seem to notice me.

'Why, Kent,' she said, walking across to where he sat. Then to Vic, 'What's the matter, doesn't he like the lovely party?'

'Sure, sure,' said Vic hastily. 'Get back to the window, baby. He'll be fine in a minute.'

She chuckled throatily.

'I'm fine now. I'm having a wonderful time.'

But she wandered unsteadily back to the window and resumed her former position. She could have been drunk, but she wasn't. She was full of something else. Something that comes in the form of white powder in little paper packets. That would account for the dilation of her eyes and her apparent indifference to the surroundings, including me. A person in that condition will only come back into the world on some strong emotional stimulation. The sight of somebody close to her, as Giovanni was, being unhappy, could lift her temporarily from the haze, but she would welcome any opportunity to drop back into it. Now she was gone again, floating on the breeze. She might well stand right where she was for hours on end. It takes different people differently.

'You make me sick, Toreno,' I said. 'The place for a thing like your brother is a padded cell. You're not telling me you didn't know he killed Wiener?'

The words stung a reply from Vic. Looking up from Giovanni's head, he said,

'You're insane. Joe knew about Little-boy's statement. We didn't dare kill him, either one of us.'

'No, I'm not insane, Vic. That blubbering mass you're holding. That's insane. Has been for years. You knew he was a killer but you did nothing to stop him. He's insane, but you're not. With me that makes you the worst of the two. Let me tell you about Giovanni, and how he came to kill Wiener.'

I walked across to the big desk and leaned over it to remove one of the big cigars I'd refused the night before. As I got close to it Toreno executed some complicated wriggling movement. When it was finished he was holding a large calibre gun in my direction.

'Sit down,' he whispered.

I shrugged, took the cigar and went back to where I'd been sitting before.

'Killing me won't solve anything,' I told him. 'The police have got it all by now anyway. They'll be here any minute. So before you get in any more trouble for his benefit, let me tell you why he killed Wiener. I got mixed up in this through your girl-friend Moira Chase.'

At mention of the name Ellen half-turned towards me, a slight frown of puzzlement on her face. Then it cleared. As she turned back to whatever she was watching she began humming something from the top twenty. The whole deal was weird.

'Moira wanted me to look into his background,' I pointed at Giovanni. 'Get something on him, and then use it to break him away from that one.' I pointed to Ellen. 'I went to the Club Coastal to take a look at him, maybe get a picture. There was a dame taking flash shots, Fay something. I talked with him, got a picture from this Fay and left. He must have asked if anybody knew me. There were one or two there who did. The hat-check girl for one. So he made his mistake. Sent Little-boy after me to rough me up and get the picture back. It didn't work, I'd already mailed it.'

The sobs were less frequent now. Evidently Giovanni was beginning to snap out of it. I went on with the story.

'So far I was nobody special. Just a guy with a long nose. Then I went out to see my client. She was there,' pointing to Ellen again. 'After I left she found out who I was and what I was up to. She also found out that I knew the probable identity of the guy who beat me up the night before. Her first thought was to tip off lover-boy here. Naturally she didn't think he'd react the way he did. May not know it even now. Giovanni headed straight for Wiener. You must have known from the first that Wiener was always danger with a big 'D'.'

Vic nodded, half to himself. Giovanni was still now, head resting on his brother's shoulder.

'Little-boy was a big tough hombre when he had a gun and a few other guys with him. Alone he was a lily. There wasn't any sand there at all. A bad-tempered man with a gun could make Wiener sing like a canary on practically any subject. If he talked to me, and I would see that he did, Giovanni was on his way to the little square room. Remember, there wasn't time for a lot of thinking. Brother-boy had to move fast. He was never the thinker around here. You had to supply all that. So he went around to Wiener's joint, maybe to warn him, maybe to tell him to take a long vacation. Who knows? Then I walked in. Just walked right in where Giovanni could give me a crack on the head. Now he was in trouble. The obvious thing was simply to kill me, but he knew Wiener would never be an accessory to murder. Little-boy was too fond of his own skin for that. It was a crisis, and Giovanni was never any good in a crisis, was he Vic? To him there was only one answer to a real problem like that. Somebody had to be killed. And in that moment of decision,

Wiener was elected and shot down even before his mind was quite made up.'

'Phooey,' said Vic, but he wasn't convincing. 'Why would Joe pull a stunt like that? He knew it was curtains for both of us if Wiener got rubbed out.'

'There was something else, something that's been working away in his mind for years. In the old days it was always the Toreno brothers. You were top man, but Joe was in there for his share. He was one of the team. Now that's all different. Only one Toreno now, and that's you. You're the glory boy, the one with the dough, the dames and the cars. The one the racket boys deal with. Joe used to be in the picture. Now he's just a back number, a guy who tags along for the ride. Somebody who is tolerated because he's a buddy of Vic Toreno's, not in his own right. He's hated it for years, I'll bet. You saved his neck with that switch back in 1957, and no doubt he was grateful enough for a while. But after a time just being alive was not enough. It began to eat at him, what a big man he'd been before he died. People looked up to him. There was that other thing too, the business with the girls. Everybody in New York was talking about Giovanni Toreno, whether they knew it or not. Now he was nothing. What'll you bet he was beginning to blame you for his troubles?'

Vic laughed shortly.

'You just don't know this family, Preston. Why, I've looked out for this boy since he was nine years old. I'd cut off my right arm for him.'

'You would?'

The words came so suddenly from Giovanni that we were both startled.

'Feeling better, huh, kid?'

'Never mind that,' Giovanni's voice was grated, and perspiration rolled freely down his face. 'Go ahead, go on.'

'Howzat? Go ahead and what?'

'Your arm. You said you'd cut it off. Go ahead.'

'Now look, Joe, that's just a way of talking — ' began Vic.

'Sure.'

Giovanni jumped up and walked about.

His steps were short and jerky and the hands that hung at his sides were clasping and unclasping.

'Just a way of talking,' he muttered. 'That's you, eh, Vic? A talker, big talker.'

'Now hold on, Joe, you're not feeling so hot . . . '

'I'm feeling great. This Preston, he's smart. I don't like him, gonna kill him in a minute, but he's smart. Got you figured, huh, Vic? The clothes, big vacations, that was you, huh?'

'Cool off, kid. You always came along.' Vic sounded worried.

'Sure, like Preston says, I was always along. For the ride. You paid the fare.'

'So?'

'So, I'm sick of it.' Giovanni's voice rose suddenly to a scream. 'Sick of it. I was always as good as you.'

'Sure you were, Joe,' said Vic soothingly. 'Every bit as good.'

'Yeah. So where's my desk? You got a desk.' He fingered the polished surface. 'Where's mine, huh? I don't see two in here. Just one. So where's mine?'

'This is plain crazy. We've been over

this. You know what we agreed.'

'No.' Giovanni's head jerked convulsively from side to side. 'No, we didn't agree nothing. You talked and I listened. You talked yourself into the top spot. You talked me out of what was mine. Oh,' he waved a hand as his brother tried to speak. 'I know what was in the back of it all. You could see that in a while I'd be taking over. I'd be the number one man. I was pretty good, you know.'

'Sure you were.'

'Don't forget it. I'm just as good now. Wiener was always trouble. I didn't have time to call you, but you know something? I wouldn't have called you if I'd had all day.'

Vic Toreno was still half-kneeling by the side of the chair his brother had just left. Now he rose to his feet, standing close to the wall, with his legs apart, like a man with something heavy on his back.

'Why wouldn't you, Joe? Why wouldn't you have called me?'

'Because I didn't need you, that's why. You fooled me too long with that stuff about Wiener's letter to the cops. Who's

Wiener? I figured it would take twenty-four hours for those New York lawyers to hear about it, and get the stuff to the D.A. Long enough for me to make Mexico with my cut. And her.'

He nodded his head towards the window, where Ellen stood in rapt concentration. Vic said, like a man in a dream,

'Let's get this straight, Joe. You knocked off Wiener and were gonna clear out and leave me to face the law by myself?'

'Why not?' grinned Giovanni. 'Big man like you, big friends. You'll only do about three years I guess. Not like sitting in that hot chair is it?'

Vic shook his head in puzzlement and sat down. He looked inexpressibly weary.

'I don't get it. The bit about Wiener, O.K. That was done in a hurry. You hole up for a while, that's fine too. I've been ready for something like this for years. I got big legal talent lined up to break anything the D.A. sets up on an old rap like that. I always figured for you to lay low for a few months, a year maybe. Without you there's no case. But this other thing, this not telling me, I'm not with that at all.'

'I been telling you why. You always heard me pretty good before. I don't need you, I can make out by myself.'

Vic Toreno looked stunned.

'So tell me something. If you figured to break for Mexico after you rubbed out Wiener, why didn't you leave right away?'

'Ah,' Giovanni's face was crafty, like a kid who's found out how to open the ice-box, 'because that's what an ordinary guy would have done. Not me, not Joe Toreno. Because I'm smart.' He tapped himself significantly on the forehead.

'There were things to do,' he continued. 'First there was Ellen. I had to talk her into coming too. She's my meal ticket until I can marry her. Then there'll be two hundred grand for me. I wasn't going to leave all that dough behind.'

'And? What else did you have to do?'

'You've forgotten, you see. No good at the detail work. It's details that make the big operators, Vic. There was the picture, the one Preston walked out with. The only picture of me that's half-way recognisable. I had to find this dame with the negative.'

'And did you?'

Giovanni suddenly lost some of his swagger. He ran his tongue round dry lips and his eyes started roaming again, as though he were looking for the door.

All this time I'd been sitting quite still, not wishing to interrupt the Torenos while they filled in the missing squares for me. Now I spoke.

'Go ahead, Giovanni. Tell Vic how smart you were with Fay.'

Vic looked at me quickly, alarm spreading across his heavy features. With some return of his old authority he said,

'Well, you heard him. What about Fay?'

Immediately Giovanni began to cringe.

'I — er, well I wanted to get — er these things — er.'

'The negatives. Yeah?'

'Called her up. She met me in a bar some place, we had a few drinks. Asked me up to her place. Look, Vic, I need a drink.'

'Like hell, you do,' shouted Vic.

He walked up to his brother and

grabbed the lapel of his jacket.

'So you went up to Fay's apartment. What's the rest?'

Giovanni averted his head to avoid looking at Vic's angry face.

'We talked. I wanted the things — the negatives — you know. Then she said we ought to get comfortable.'

'Oh, no,' breathed Vic, 'no.'

At once Giovanni gabbled out the rest of it, as though explaining some misdemeanour to the teacher.

'She took off some of her clothes. Started fooling around. You know, the way they do. She kept wanting me to do — things. I kept asking her to stop, Vic, honest, but she laughed at me. Thought it was a gag, thought I was kidding. She kept on and on, I couldn't stand it, you know I can't stand that, Vic. There was this knife I'd seen in the kitchen. It was like the other times, Vic. You know, I didn't mean her any harm; but she wouldn't leave me alone. Finally she started shouting at me, calling me names. Bad things. I had to stop her, Vic, you can see that. I couldn't have her say these things to me. It was like the other times. The bad times. I couldn't help it. You know I had to shut her up, had to stop her calling me those bad names.'

It was all out in a torrent. While he talked Giovanni was plucking at Vic's shirt with his fingers as if anxious to establish contact, eager to be reassured. Vic's head was sunk low on his shoulders. Now he released his grip on Giovanni, patted him on the shoulder. Like a parent reproving a wayward child he said,

'You oughtn't to have done that to Fay.'

'No.' Giovanni's face was working jerkily, his eyes staring so much they seemed likely to bulge from their sockets. 'No, I didn't mean her any harm, Vic. You know I didn't.'

'You heard enough, Toreno?' I asked.

'Shut up, I've got to think,' he replied.

'Not much time for that. You might have got away with your original idea if everything stayed the way it was. But with him killing Fay in the same way he killed those others, the law can establish similarity. Whether they find him or not they'll know he's not dead. And they'll have you.'

'Shut up, will you?' snarled Vic.

'I'll make a deal with you. Come with me to the police and we'll both turn him in. You might get off with a very light sentence.'

'Will you for crissakes shut up!' he bellowed.

'I'll shut him up, Vic. I'll make him stop for you.'

Giovanni was about six feet from me. He stuck a hand in his pocket. When he brought it out there was a click and four inches of steel sprang from between his fingers. He smiled at me.

'You've been lucky. Police should have locked you up for killing Little-boy.'

'I'm lucky,' I agreed, watching his face carefully. 'When they do put me away it'll be in a cell. Not a room with padded walls.'

'You shouldn't talk to me that way,' he scowled. 'There's nothing wrong with me.'

'Except you're crazy in the head,' I sneered. 'You're stark raving mad, Giovanni. What's the matter, don't you know what to do with a woman?'

With a high-pitched scream he flung himself the distance between us, the switch-blade stuck out in front of him like a bayonet. Vic shouted for him to stop but it was too late then. I dived sideways to the floor taking the chair with me. Giovanni couldn't check himself. As the chair toppled over his feet hit the protruding legs and he went face-down with a crash. I was half-way to my feet now, clinging to the top of the desk as I levered myself up. My back was to Giovanni for that one moment, and I felt the cold sweat break out all over me in the second before I was able to turn and face him. He was just getting up from the floor, clumsily, pushing at the carpet with both hands, like a man doing press-ups. He fell forward again at the first attempt. I didn't take my eyes off him, but I knew his brother hadn't moved. Giovanni was on his knees now, back to me, crying weakly, and seemed to be plucking at his stomach. He half-stood half-kneeled, turning slowly towards me. His face was grey and the unheeded tears streamed over his cheeks. His breathing was deep and fast. When he got almost round I could see the knife. It was just above the waist-band of his pants. I hadn't seen the handle before. It was an ornate piece of carved white ivory. The four-inch blade was planted firmly in his stomach, thin rivulets of blood running from it. Using his hands in attempting to break the fall, he must have pointed the knife towards himself as he hit the floor.

There was disbelief written large on the ashen features. He was dying as he stood there. Feebly he grasped the handle and tried to tug it out. It would have made no difference if he could have, there was death in his eyes already.

'Joe.'

Vic Toreno was across the room in a rush. Giovanni held out a hand towards his as if for support. Before Vic could reach him a great gout of blood spurted suddenly from his mouth and this time he went down to stay. For a moment the surviving Toreno stood staring helplessly down at his brother's body. Then he knelt gently beside the blood-spattered corpse, whispering to him in soft tones. Stroking the lifeless head and patting the shoulder. He looked up and saw me standing there. Waiting.

'This is yours, shamus. You son-of-a-bitch.'

'Wait, Toreno — ' I began.

But he didn't wait. The big .45 was clear of his pocket and coming up level with my body. I plucked the little derringer from my sleeve. Vic saw it but took no notice. By the time the derringer was pointing in the right direction I was staring down the vast black hole in front of the revolver. There was a sharp crack from the tiny weapon in my hand as I eased on the trigger. The slug hit him slightly off-centre of the forehead, spinning him round. The thunderous roar from the .45 was a split second late. The heavy slug tore a great gash in the desk by my left leg. As Vic fell backwards across his prostrate brother the gun went off again and a large hole appeared in the ceiling.

There was a crash as the door was flung open. Al came in at the run, a blue automatic in his hand. The derringer is a single shot pistol.

'Wait,' I shouted desperately, dropping my gun on the floor.

He paused uncertainly, taking in the two corpses at a glance. At that moment Ellen Chase came from behind me. The shots must have had some effect on her addled brain.

'Kent,' she screamed, flinging herself towards the body of her late boy-friend.

I went after her, grabbing her round the waist and pulling her away. It was all up to Al now.

'Listen, Al,' I tried to sound confident, 'this set-up is cold. Nothing you do with that is going to change anything. Vic's gone, and without him the Alhambra is all washed-up.' He was listening anyway, that was a start.

'You're not going to win any medals knocking me off. As it stands your nose is clean in this town. Leave it rest.'

It was clear he was thinking about it.

'About Vic,' he said, 'you kill him?'

'I had to. This other guy rubbed himself out, fell on the knife. Then Vic pulled out this cannon. He was going to kill us both.'

Ellen was heavy in my arms. She must have passed out cold.

'Who's the dame?' came the question.

'To you she's two centuries in hard cash. Are you listening?'

'I'm listening.'

'She shouldn't be here. This has nothing to do with her. Toreno's buddy filled her full of happy dust. She don't even know what day it is. Take her home, I'll phone and say you're bringing her. She was never here, you got that?'

'Tell me the bit about the two c's again.'

'You get it when she's safe at home.'

'Suppose the coppers know she was here?'

'They don't.'

'Well suppose they find out?'

'You're breaking my heart. You'll tell 'em they're mistaken. You've never seen her before.'

Al decided suddenly, and stuck the gun out of sight in his jacket pocket. I felt relieved. He jabbed a thumb at the sprawled corpses on the floor.

'Who cleans up the store?' he demanded.

'The police. It's their job. All you boys here are clean on this. The whole thing was between the Torenos and me.'

'Torenos? You mean the piano-player was a relative of Vic's?'

I nodded.

'Some. No time for talk now. Get the girl out of here.'

I told him the address. When he heard it his eyes narrowed.

'Fancy address, huh? Make it a quarter.'

'All right, you thief, a quarter. Now get going.'

He half-dragged Ellen across to the door and out. Suddenly I found my whole body was shaking violently. It could have been an early fever symptom but it wasn't. It was plain crawling fear. Two people had been about to kill me in the last ten minutes. By any reasonable average, one of them should have made it. I lit a cigarette with trembling hands.

A drink seemed to be a good idea. There was a half-full bottle of bourbon set up on a tray with some soda and glasses. I helped myself to a generous measure and swallowed half of it down at one gulp. Then I sat down in Toreno's chair beyond the big desk to wait for Rourke.

10

There's a framed photograph of a middle-aged Irish-looking woman and two pretty teenage girls on the desk in Lieutenant John Rourke's office. He's a strong family man, likes to have a picture of what he calls his three girl-friends around the office. I wasn't talking to the family man. I was talking to Rourke the Captain of Detectives of the Monkton City Police Force. Had been talking almost three hours, off and on.

' — I felt I needed a drink. So I poured one and waited for you,' I concluded.

'And that's all?' he queried, gimlet-eyes boring into my face. 'That's the whole story?'

'That's all.'

'I like it.' He nodded reflectively, ejecting a cloud of foul smoke across the table towards me. 'I like it fine. It's a nice story. Got a little of everything, little sex-appeal, everything. Tell it to me again.'

I sighed. It was hot in the small stuffy room. After the fourteenth time I'd given up keeping count of the number of times I'd told the story.

'How many more times, Rourke?' I asked.

Somebody grabbed my shoulder hard and half-spun me out of the chair.

'Preston, we like you here. It's very dull, police work. A good story helps to pass the time. You heard the captain. Tell it again.'

I stared balefully into Gil Randall's heavy face.

'This woman came to see me — '

'What woman?'

'Mrs. Moira Chase.'

'Chase? Would she be related to F. Harper Chase?'

And we were off again.

It was seven in the evening when Rourke thrust a wad of close-typed sheets under my nose.

'Read it, sign it, get out,' he told me.

I read it. It was O.K. I picked up the pen.

'All three copies,' he insisted.

I would have signed away every nickel I ever had for the promise of getting out of that room. Not that I'd been pushed around physically. Just the ceaseless probing barrage of questions had left my mind like seaweed. Randall had quit half an hour before and Rourke and I were alone.

'You think I ought to try for an indictment?' he queried.

I thought about it.

'Maybe,' I shrugged. 'What charge?'

'You tell me.'

'Murder Three?' I hazarded.

Rourke nodded.

'Yupp.' He tapped at the typed statement. 'On your version of the Vic Toreno killing, I think I might swing an indictment for Murder Three against you.'

'Are you going to?'

He snorted.

'Where would it get me? Indictment, yeah, fine. But it's convictions and sentences that count. Half the legal talent in the state is lined up on your side already. All I'd wind up with would be sore ears listening to the Chief telling me about wasting the public funds.'

The part about the legal talent was intriguing.

'What legal talent?' I asked.

'Oh, you wouldn't know about that, huh? Well downstairs now are two different sets of lawyers. One bunch sent by Mrs. Chase, the other by Marsland Freeman the Second. I never saw so many lawyers. Been here since four this afternoon most of 'em.'

'Trying to get me out?'

'Not exactly. They could have got you out right away if you'd been under interrogation or anything. But when I explained you were feeling beat and were just resting in my office they said they'd wait.'

So I could have gone free hours before.

'Thanks,' I said bitterly.

'Don't be that way, Preston. I wasn't satisfied at the time. May have been something wrong with your yarn. We hadn't been over it enough times.'

'Well, I hope you're satisfied now.'

'I think so. It all worked out pretty

much as I figured.'

I laughed shortly.

'As you figured? You're not trying to tell me you had all this mapped out from the beginning? Because if you are, Lieutenant, I don't believe you.'

He waved a deprecating hand.

'Oh no, no. Not the details. Like the brother, now. I didn't know about him. No, let me tell you exactly what I did have in mind.'

'Do,' I said tersely.

He leaned back in the hard wooden chair and stared at the solitary swinging lamp.

'Here I am in Monkton. They call me Captain of Detectives. That means I'm supposed to take an interest in people who break the law. Along comes this Toreno and opens a gambling joint right in my territory. What would you say the police should do?'

'Close him up, I guess.'

'That's very good, very good. Yeah, we should close him up. But what do we find? Toreno has friends. Not just any old friends, but most of the important people for miles around. With Freeman's money and influence, and all the politicos who won't have any disrepute brought on the name of the late F. Harper Chase through any friend of his widow getting in trouble, we run up against opposition. Hands off Toreno. I was thinking of raising a public subscription to erect a monument to the guy as a local hero, when suddenly I got a little break. You.'

'How come?'

'Suddenly one of Toreno's business associates becomes dead, and you're holding the baby. Now, at the time, I didn't know for sure whether you killed him or not. But you were in it up to here, and that was all I needed.'

'All right.' I was interested in spite of myself. 'Suppose I had killed him. What then?'

'Then Toreno would have to do something about you. If you were arrested, O.K., let the law do it. But if I put you back on the street, Toreno has to even the score, or try. That's when I would have been waiting for him.'

'You sent me out to be a clay pigeon?' I

stuttered with rage.

'Sort of. On the other hand suppose you didn't do it. I know you. You'd go pushing your nose in everything, something may come up I could use.'

'And something did,' I observed sourly.

'Something did. Now I'm rid of Toreno. And the Alhambra Club. I haven't stepped on anybody's toes. The Department rating with the politicians and what have you remains high. Everybody satisfied.'

'Everybody but me,' I reminded him. 'I damn near got my head shot off today.'

'Tck tck,' he clicked sympathetically. 'That would have been rough. My heart bleeds for you. Let me put you straight on something, Preston. I'd rather see six of you get knocked off than one uniformed officer who's just trying to keep the peace. I know all about your fancy fees. What you'll get paid for a couple of days' work ought to be fair compensation for any inconvenience you might have been put to.'

'Thanks for being so worried about me,' I told him.

'Tell me one thing, Preston,' he went on. 'Every time I tried to turn any heat on Toreno I ran into a concrete wall ten feet thick, donated by Marsland Freeman II. You come along and spatter Toreno's brains all over the floor, suddenly Freeman weighs in on your side. What did you do to him? I mean what made him change sides that way?'

'You don't know?' I queried. I was thinking of Littleboy Wiener's affidavit. The New York police had had time by now to contact our local force. It seemed to me Rourke was playing cat and mouse.

'How would I know?' he returned. 'The name Freeman doesn't appear anywhere in your statement.'

'I don't know of any connection between Freeman and Toreno,' I said.

'Why Freeman is on my side is because his daughter and I have been seeing each other. For all I know he may not even be aware that I'm in here. Lois may have sent all the legal talent down on her own say-so.'

'Rourke pursed his lips together thoughtfully.

'Do tell?' he said. 'They say she's an eyeful. You seem to do all right, Preston.'

'Don't I though? Well, if that's all, I'll be getting along.'

'Go ahead. This is the nearest we came to being on the same team in quite a while. Make a habit of it.'

From Rourke that was the equivalent of a banquet-in-honour-of from anybody else. I grinned.

'See you at the inquest, Lieutenant.'

★ ★ ★

A week later I was sitting in my office pretending to be working. The inquest on the Toreno brothers had taken place the day before and the papers had used it to give the whole story a dying kick. There was a good head-and-shoulders of Ellen Chase, the lovely girl who had innocently spent a whole day in the company of a depraved murderer, and who had left a hospital bed to do her civic duty at the hearing, etc., etc.

I was glad about Ellen. Moira had pushed her straight into an expensive sanatorium as soon as she heard about the drugs. Ellen, it seemed, was new to the game and should be cured within a few weeks. If everything went well, that was. I never saw the doctor who would put a hand on his heart and swear any single patient was cured for good. But Ellen was young and, most important, extrovert. There was no reason why she should ever feel a need for artificial stimulation of that kind. Moira had come through one hundred per cent. When action was called for she had been right up there in front. After Al had delivered Ellen back to her home Moira took over at that end. Within hours there was a sanatorium reservation for her stepdaughter, two hundred and fifty dollars in small bills paid to Al, a batch of lawyers sent to police headquarters to get me off the hook. She even deposited five hundred dollars in my name at the bank in case I needed funds in a hurry. Moira was quite a gal.

During the past week I had also managed to find out how it was Rourke couldn't explain Marsland Freeman's interest in Vic Toreno. Reason was he didn't know anything about it. The contact came in all right from New York but it was channelled to somebody high up in the city administration. You don't get to be high up in the city administration without knowing where your duty lies. The official had gone to his boss, who went to his boss. His boss was somebody close to Marsland Freeman II, and as the millionaire was not taking business calls right then, the matter was left lying on the table. By the time Freeman became available the story was finished, and there was no point in anybody raking over any mud which would embarrass the great man. So the business was forgotten, and even if I didn't approve of the way it came about, I had to admit it was probably the best solution from all points of view.

When I first received the cheque that came in from one of the law firms who acted as agents for Freeman, I thought about sending it back. It was, to say the least of it, a ridiculous figure for what I'd done. Especially since I hadn't been working for him at the time. Greed got the better of me in the end, naturally. I always admire these high-principled characters on the movies who drop the stolen money in the sea, or light a cigarette with a fat cheque. Great gestures. But it takes a great man to make a great gesture. After a few hours of indecision, what I did was to deposit that cheque in the name of Mark Preston at the Monkton City Branch of the United National Bank. I still had a feeling I had no moral right to the money, but the bank teller didn't ask me that. He just read the amount and the signature and gave me a great wide smile.

It was a few minutes before noon and I was trying to decide whether to spend the afternoon lazing at the beach, when the door opened. I didn't look up. It had to be Miss Digby, because nobody ever got past her desk.

'Reading about what a hero you are?'

I looked up fast then. Lois Freeman was in white today. A strapless beach dress that permitted her to do most of her sun bathing without taking it off. I caught my breath. She stood across the desk from me, very straight and very beautiful.

She wore no jewellery, nothing to detract from the endowments lavished on her by nature. She was smiling. I found I was smiling too.

'My father thinks you were pretty damned wonderful,' she told me.

'Your father's opinion was deposited in the bank on Monday,' I replied.

'I think you were pretty damned wonderful too. I haven't brought my cheque-book with me,' she said evenly.

'All right, I'm sorry. Maybe I shouldn't have said that. But you worry me. That night at the Alhambra, O.K. I could buy that. But the next morning out at your house, that seemed to be less family business and more Lois business. Now the family business is all over. Now you show again. It makes me nervous.'

'I don't see why it should. Men get all kinds of reactions, I've found, but I don't usually make them nervous. Not the way you mean.'

She was not going to quarrel with me unless I made it so.

'Look,' I realised I always seemed to be asking her to look, 'you're out of my league. I can't keep up with you, don't want to try. You like the look of me for a while. How long? I just mixed in something which turned out to be your business. Now your sister doesn't need to be hidden away any more. I am responsible, that makes me some kind of a hero, the boy who made the eighty-yard touchdown. But it's momentary. It'll pass.'

The tawny head moved from side to side slowly, definitely.

'You're mistaken. You spend too much time with your psychoanalyst. I'm here. Period.'

I pushed the newspapers in a heap to one side of the desk and searched around for cigarettes. Then I stood up to lean across to light the one Lois held. She looked into my eyes over the flame of the lighter. She was very tall, only about three inches below my own height. I took the cigarette from between her lips and kissed her gently. I couldn't do much else with the desk between us.

'That was nice. Much better,' she acknowledged.

'Better than what?'

'The other time, in the car.'

'I liked it fine in the car,' I protested.

'Yes, so did I. It was good, but this was better. This went much further down.'

When I don't know what a woman's talking about I always keep quiet. It was as well, because her next remark came at a dizzy angle.

'There's a lake outside San Diego.'

'Huh? There's lots of lakes outside San Diego.'

'Not like this one. This one has the largest moon in the world attached.'

'I'm not going to say anything,' I said slowly, 'because you haven't finished yet, have you?'

'No. The lake is small. There's a cabin there, twenty miles to the nearest store. It's a wonderful place to fish, swim or just laze around.'

'And you own it,' I made it a statement.

'I own it,' she nodded.

Then she opened her purse and put something down on the desk between us. It was a heavy old-fashioned key.

'My car is outside. We could be there

inside three hours. We'd need a few things, food, cigarettes and so on. You'll have to get them. I haven't got a red cent with me.'

I weighed the key thoughtfully in my hand.

'You're sure about this?'

She nodded gravely.

'I'm sure. I'd have preferred it to be your idea but — '

'Don't talk like that. This was my idea from the start. I just didn't want to frighten you away.'

'Then that's settled.' Almost timidly she added, 'You — you know why I haven't brought any money with me, don't you?'

'Yes. Because I'm a bigoted neurotic who can't see further than his own nose.'

We grinned. At the door of the outer office I said,

'Oh, Miss Digby, I'm enquiring into a matter for a friend of Miss Freeman's. In San Diego.'

'Very well, Mr. Preston,' said Florence. 'When may I expect you back?'

'Kind of hard to say. May take quite a while.'

She looked at Lois, then me.

'I see.'

They must have heard her sniff at the far end of the corridor.

THE END

We do hope that you have enjoyed reading this large print book.

Did you know that all of our titles are available for purchase?

We publish a wide range of high quality large print books including:
**Romances, Mysteries, Classics
General Fiction
Non Fiction and Westerns**

Special interest titles available in large print are:
**The Little Oxford Dictionary
Music Book, Song Book
Hymn Book, Service Book**

Also available from us courtesy of Oxford University Press:
**Young Readers' Dictionary
(large print edition)
Young Readers' Thesaurus
(large print edition)**

For further information or a free brochure, please contact us at:
**Ulverscroft Large Print Books Ltd.,
The Green, Bradgate Road, Anstey,
Leicester, LE7 7FU, England.
Tel:** (00 44) **0116 236 4325
Fax:** (00 44) **0116 234 0205**

Other titles in the
Linford Mystery Library:

DEATH CALLED AT NIGHT

R. A. Bennett

Jimmy Ellis believes his parents have died in a car crash when as a young boy he is taken to live with relatives in Australia. The years pass happily, then the nightmare comes. Terrifying images flit through his mind in the dark — all through the eyes of a child, a witness to grisly events seventeen years before. He begins to delve into the past, and soon he finds himself on the trail of a double murderer — a murderer who is prepared to kill again.

THE DEAD TALE-TELLERS

John Newton Chance

Jonathan Blake always kept appointments. He had kept many, in all sorts of places, at all sorts of times, but never one like that one he kept in the house in the woods in the fading light of an October day. It seemed a perfect, peaceful place to visit and perhaps take tea and muffins round the fire. But at this appointment his footsteps dragged, for he knew that inside the house the men with whom he had that date were already dead . . .

THREE DAYS TO LIVE

Robert Charles

Mike Harrigan was scar-faced, a drifter, and something of a woman-hater. With his partner Dan Barton he searched the upper reaches of the Rio Negro in the treacherous rain forests of Brazil, lured by a fortune in uncut emeralds. Behind them rode three killers who believed that they had already found the precious stones. And then fate handed Harrigan not emeralds, but the lives of women, three of them nuns, and trapped them all in a vast series of underground caverns.